A CLANCY RYAN NOVEL

JAMES FERGUSON

ISBN
978-1-77839-057-9 (Paperback)
978-1-77839-058-6 (eBook)

The New Doctor

Table of Contents

Chapter 1

Most people would think that Clancy Ryan was nothing more than a big dumb Irish man. He was big, standing a little over 6' 3" and weighting in at 235 pounds of hard muscle earned by years of weight training and running. He was Irish, right down to his sandy red hair and easy-going ways. But to think Clancy Jameson Ryan dumb was a mistake many a would be law breaker had lived to regret.

Clancy Ryan was the sheriff of MacAbee County, Illinois. County seat, MacAbee.population just under 4500 people. The good sheriff was something of a local hero around the county having starred at every sport offered at school before going on to the University of Florida on a football scholarship. There he started at strong side linebacker until he was blindsided by a 350-pound lineman in the Auburn game. His playing days were over. He had a ruptured lower lumbar disk which required surgery to repair.

Clancy had thought he'd end up in pro football, but after the surgery he decided to find a safer means of making a living. He red shirted his senior year, got his degree in Economics with a minor in political science and left school and football behind.

After Florida he went to Georgetown University and earned a Master's degree in criminal justice. He thought about law school but didn't want to spend the rest of his life arguing.

He was thirty-four years old, single, never even close to the alter. Every single woman in MacAbee between the ages of 15 to 50 had their eyes on Clancy. He was well liked and had just been re-elected to a second term as sheriff.

It was a cold rainy morning early September as Clancy pulled his Yukon County squad car into his spot at the court house. Not in the best of moods, he'd hoped to make it to his office without having to see anyone. No such luck. Standing in the doorway, apparently waiting for him was Mayor Toms. His full name was Thomas Thomas, thus Toms.

"Good morning Mayor."

"Good morning Clancy. Weather turning colder today."

Not wanting to stand out in the rain Clancy said, "Is there something I can do for you."

"Well." Said the mayor "I just wanted to make sure were going to make our little brunch today."

"The one for the new doctor." said Clancy.

"That's the one. One o'clock at Millie's."

"I'll be there." Clancy said with a sigh of resignation.

Mayor Tom's was 5'6" in shoes that some say had lifts, so he had to reach up over his head just to pat Clancy on the shoulder.

"What's the matter Clancy. You look tired."

"Oh you know. Another dust up out at Rollie's last night."

"Bikers and farmhands again?" asked the mayor.

"Of course." said Clancy "Farmhands work 8 to 10 hours a day all week, Friday's payday. They're just looking for a place where they can blow off some steam, get a few beers and relax. Some even brought dates. The bikes sit around all day, drinking and smoking whatever, hygiene optional. By the time the farm boys get there the bikers are bored and looking for trouble."

"What started it this time?

"Same thing that always starts it," Said Clancy. "Some biker chick gets up close to a clean young farm boy, fatter, older smellier biker not liking it. If you ask me it was a setup. If you're looking for a fight, what better way to start one? I got two of the bikers, the women who started it and Willie Johns is on in jail right.

I could find a neutral witness maybe I could charge someone for something. "Willie again".said the mayor. "When will that boy grow up?"

"Never."said Clancy. As he started to head for his office. He got tree steps before the mayor stopped him.

"One more thing Clancy" he said. "I need you to pick up our new doctor for the brunch, ok, one o'clock at the doctor's office."

Not wanting to argue Clancy said, "Fine." and walked off.

Chapter 2

The doctor in question was Dr. Rebecca Whitmore. A graduate of John Hopkins Med school by way of Boston College, she was a first rate general practitioner with training in forensics and pathology.

She'd been recruited by old Doc Hamilton as his replacement. He'd announced that after fifty-one years as the towns only doctor, he was finally retiring.

Some were a little surprised that she took the job. Well educated, top of her class with a good position at a first rate Chicago hospital and a nice apartment off Halsted in the University Village part of the south side area that used to be the Maxwell street open arket, a notorious free market where one could buy almost anything.

She had saved enough money so she could put a down payment on one of the nice condos going up all over the place.

She was living the good life.

What nobody outside her immediate family and a few colleges at the hospital knew was that Dr. Rebecca Whitmore was nearly beating to death one night while she waited for a bus.

Twice a week she volunteered at Cook County Hospital's emergency room, which kept her out late. That night as she waited for the bus, she was jumped from behind.

The first thing she feared was getting raped until she saw that the gang was a group of teen age girls.

They took her money, her jewelry and even her shoes before beating unconscious and left for dead.

Rebecca Whitmore spent six weeks in the hospital, two more in rehab after which she went home to Boston.

Her boss at the hospital told her to take all the time she needed, but she knew that no amount of time was going to put her back to where she was. Her parents wanted her

to stay in Boston. Her father was a prominent surgeon and was on the board of directors at Boston General. Surly he could find her a good position somewhere.

After two months at home, Rebecca was ready to bolt when a call came from the head of her hospital in Chicago. An old friend from med school had called him looking for a young doctor to take over his practice in a rural town south of Chicago and would Rebecca be interested.

"The perfect way to ease back into working," he'd said. "Maybe you could stay a year or so."

Rebecca jumped at the chance. She first flew to Chicago to settle her affairs there, packed all she owned into a rented mini-van and headed out into the middle of nowhere.

Rebecca had called ahead and talked to Dr, Hamilton about the clinic. She'd also made arrangements at the local B&B for a room until she could make a more permanent arrangement.

Doctors Hamilton and Whitmore had talked for more then an hour as Rebecca drove south towards MacAbee, Ill. She had found Dr. Hamilton warm and encouraging and she liked him immediately.

She had asked Dr. Hamilton not to make a fuss about her coming. He said he'd try, but her coming was already the talk of town. She was mildly upset about today's luncheon even though she understood why it was necessary. She put it out of her mind and went about her first day on the new job, thinking this might just work out.

Chapter 3

Are you ever gonna let me out of here." Bellowed Jake Tuner, the biker how for the most part was the instigator of the fight at Rollies last night. He'd been yelling and screaming ever since he'd woke up with what had to be a huge hangover and a badly beat up face.

Jake Tuner had pushed the wrong farm boy to be his dance partner. Willie Johnson was younger by 15 years, in far better shape and just as willing to go a few rounds as Jake. But unlike Jake, Willie was just lying on his bunk waiting to go home. It wasn't the first time Willie had seen the inside of the MacAbee county jail.

The Johnson Family owned the best part of MacAbee farmland and were done to earth people. Willie was not. He liked his whiskey and his women to much to suite his father Jack or his grandfather Old Horace Johnson who was the real power in the county.

Willie wasn't a bad guy nor a trouble maker by choice, just a guy who seemed to always be in the wrong place at the wrong time.

Willie and Clancy had gone to school together and were what you'd call friends. If only Willie could stay out of places like Rollies on Friday nights and the county jail Saturday mornings.

"I'm gonna sue this rat hole of a town if I don't get out of here soon." Screamed Turner.

"You got nothing on me. Willie boy here started it."

"Will you shut up." Yelled Tom Thomas Jr, the mayor own son and current chief deputy. "Old Judge Pennybrook will be in at ten o'clock. You'll just have to wait till then. Don't worry asshole; you'll be out by noon."

"Until then, why don't I put you and Willie in the same cell and go get me a donut. What do you sat Willie, up for a rematch," This got Willie up. He walked slowly towards the bars between the cells and said, "Don't mind if I do."

Tuner was big and dumb but he knew when he was being set up. Whenever an outsider went against a local, the outsider always lost. It had been that way ever since Jake and his brother Jimmy had started riding years ago.

"Your time will come Willie Boy. We'll be looking for you later. You'll see when Jimmy gets back. You'll see, and where's my wife.'

"We got a special part of the jail for ladies," smirked Toms Jr. "But we let her use it anyways." Willie couldn't help but laugh, which made Turner madder then hell.

"We'll see farm boy. We'll see,"

Chapter 4

At ten o'clock as the contenders were being led into Judge Pennybrook's courtroom, Rebecca was up to her elbows in patients.

"Is it always like this?" She asked Dr. Hamilton, 'Is there an epidemic you failed to tell me about."

"No," said the doc "People just want to get a look at you. You'd have to be almost fifty years old to say I didn't have a hand in bringing you into this world."

"Dr. Whitmore," called the day nurse, Jean Winston, "Phone call, it's the mayor."I'll take it in the study Jean."

She closed the door, took a deep breath, picked up the phone and said, "Good morning Mayor Thomas."

Good morning Dr. Whitmore and please call me Toms."

"Toms?"

"You know Tom Thomas plural thus Toms."

"Right, you ok with that."

"Why not, makes me seem homey to the voters."

"OK, Toms, what can I do for you?"

"Just calling to see how things are going and to remind you of our little get together this afternoon."

Rebecca let out a sigh and said" Things are a little hectic here today. I might not get out of here till Thursday. Seems the whole county has the got to see the new doctor flu"

Don't you worry Dr. Whitmore, Dr. Hamilton assures me that the office will be empty by 12:00 noon and that he'll close up and send the sight seers home. I've made arrangements to have our Sheriff Ryan pick you up at 12:45."

"The sheriff, why the sheriff."

"To tell the truth, it's the only way I could think of to make sure he'd be there."

"Why, is he hard to get along with?"

"Sometimes, yes he is, but mostly he's a great guy, well liked by everywhere. It's just that he goes his own way, kind of a loner."

"And he got elected sheriff?"

"Twice." Said the mayor. "Largest voter turn-out ever. Un-apposed. I think anyone who could vote did, for him."

"Yet you feel the need to trick him into coming to the brunch."

"Let's not call it a trick. Let's call it insurance. So we'll see you at one o'clock then."

"Sure Mr. Mayor, I'll be there."

After she had hung up the phone Rebecca went looking for Jean the nurse.

"The mayor got the sheriff to assort me to the luncheon. Is that normal?"

"The mayor is always trying to boss the sheriff around. It almost never works. Must want a look at you for him self."

"Oh great, Dr of medicine or a prize hog."

"Doctor, Jean said sternly, "Around here a prize hog is a big deal."

"I'm sorry, I, I didn't mean..."

It's ok. Most people around here just country folks, set in there ways. The sheriff is no different. Wait till you meet him. You'll see. He's probably the counties most eligible bachelor."

"This just keeps getting better. The mayor wouldn't be trying to set me up would he?"

Na, even the mayor wouldn't stoop that low and the sheriff isn't someone you'd want mad at you. And don't read too much into that 'Most Eligible Bachelor' thing. That just means he's one of a handful of single guys left in the county with a visible means of support."

"Thanks Rebecca said, Or, heaven forbid, we miss the big party."

Chapter 5

At about the same time Dr. Whitmore was resuming her rounds, the festivities at the courthouse were in full bloom. Judge Pennybrook was about to dismiss all charges, against the strong opposition of the County Attorney, Mike Billings.

"But your Honor, Mr. Turner and his gang have terrorized this community ever since they got here. Don't you think its time to send a message to them that we're not going to let them take over our town?"

Mr., Billings," The judge spoke slowly but was always to the point," If you had one witness, other then those involved, then you might have a case."

"But your Honor."

"No buts Mr. Billings. Mr. Johnson's father has already seen to the damages and Mr. Steins didn't bother to show up this morning, so you have no case."

With that the judge pounded his gavel and said, "Case dismissed."

"Damn right," yelled Jake Turner. High fiving the biker around him who had come to see the show. The judge looked up, pounded his gavel again and said. "That will be one hundred dollars contempt of court Mr. Turner, for profanity in my court. Pay the clerk or the sheriff can take you back to your second home in out fine jail."

"I got it Jake." Said the ugliest man Clancy had ever seen.

From his perch at the back of the room, Clancy was for the most part the de-factor sergeant-at-arms during any court proceedings. As Turner and his group headed for the, Clancy stood ramrod straight, blocking their way.

"One day joke, you're going to screw up, and when you do I'll be there to mop you up."

"What'd a mean sheriff, Judge just said I was a law abiding citizen."

"Right, we'll be seeing you soon joke."

With that said Clancy turned and walked away.

Chapter 6

Clancy was back in his office when Mike Billings stuck his head in and said, "You got a minute Clancy."

"Sure Mike. Sit down. I got to go to that luncheon for the new Doc at one o'clock.
 I even have to pick her up."

"Really," said Mike, "I here she's damn good looking."

"So, the mayor's making sure I show up, that all. What can I do for you, Mike?"

"I wanted to talk to you about the Turner Brothers. Sooner or later we're going to have to rid this town of that vermin."

"I know, we're trying. That's the third time we've had Jake in court and the third time he's walked. At least Jimmy is up at Joliet for now."

When's he due to get out."

"Soon, unfortunately."

"All we ever get Jake on is pity things like fighting. You know as well as I do they're running drugs. Since they've showed up there's been more weed and meth in the county then ever. That can't be a coincidence."

"I know, we've looked everywhere we can think and nothing."

"Somewhere in this county or close by, these boys are running a meth lab. Have you checked with Edger over in Crabtree County?"

"According to Edger, Crabtree County has no drug problem so why should he waist his manpower looking for something that's not there."

"Great," moaned the C.A. "With thinking like that we'll never find anything.

What about Jimmy"

"Well, He's due to get out of Joliet in two weeks. I'm assuming he's coming here. Jake's to dumb to run things, Jimmy was always the brains. Once he gets back things should quite down. Jimmy doesn't like high profiles."

"Plus he's going to be on parole forever."

Alice, the police dispatcher knocked on the door and said. "Mayor Toms is on line one for you Sheriff."

"I did, told me to get you anyway."

Chapter 7

Clancy held up a finger to tell Mike not to say anything, shook his head and picked up the phone.

"Mr. Mayor, what can I do for you now?"

"Just checking in. Making sure we're all set for this afternoon." Said the mayor in what most people call his "sing song" voice. The one he trots out during an election year.

Tom you're aware I have a master's degree from Georgetown University in Washington D.C."

"Yes, but…"

"And that I'm the duly elected sheriff of MacAbee County, while you are only the mayor of one town. I think if you add that up, I out rank you."

Mike Billings was doing his best not to burst out laughing.

"Now Clancy, no need for you to get nasty. It's just a luncheon. It'll be good for You. All of the counties most powerful people well be there."

"I'll be there." Clancy said as he hung up the phone without so much as a 'good-bye.

He looked back at Mike who was smiling like a kid on Christmas morning.

"What." Snarled Clancy.

"Nothing, nothing. Got the same speech about twenty minutes ago."

"Well he's persistent."

"Mayor Toms delivers." Said Mike quoting the mayors most recent campaign slogan.

"I've got to run out to the Johnson's farm before the big show. I missed Will at court today."

"Still beating that dead horse." Said Mike.

"Look, You, me and Will go back a long way, both of us owe him a lot."

"I know, we were like brothers back in High school."

"He was married to my sister; he's the father of my nephew Jack."

"If I recall you were going to cut his heart out when he got Leddie pregnant and that marriage was over before it got started."

"Yea well, I still feel like I should do something. Why don't you come along?

We'll blow off the luncheon; go fishing just like old times."

"Can't, got an appointment with Judge Pennybrook. He wants to chew on me a little before I escort him to party."

"Mayor Toms?"

"Mayor Toms."

They both stood up laughing. Clancy grabbed Mike by the shoulder and said, "Looks like I got the better assignment."

"You got the bigger gun."

"I'll bet you a steak dinner your wife got to the mayor and set this up."

"No bet." Laughed Mike, "Her one and only goal in life is to see you married off. Preferable a local girl, but why waist a golden opportunity."

"So you're in on this too."

"No sir, not me."

Chapter 8

The Johnson place was big, almost three thousand acres of corn and soybeans.

Their main business was dairy and livestock, having the market cornered in county stud services.

As Clancy parked his squad car up by the main house, he saw Old Horace standing with Neil Johnson, Will's dad and Thom Billings, Mike's uncle. They were having what can only be called a great big argument. All three men looked up as Clancy got out of his car, Neil Johnson and Thom Billings walked away in different directions.

"Good morning Sheriff,"

"Good Morning Horace." Said Clancy. He'd always thought of Old Horace as a kind of a father figure. He'd known him all his life and since Will had married his sister and produced young Jack they were family.

"Not very popular today am I." said Clancy.

"Oh don't mind them. Just a little disagreement between friends. So what can I do for you this morning?"

"I'm looking for Will. Has he come back yet?"

"Will? Haven't seen him since yesterday afternoon. I thought you had him."

"I did but the judge sent him packing."

"How is the old judge?" "Fine. Still cranky as hell but in good health. What about Will?"

"Haven't seen him. Needed him here today to. Not in anymore trouble is he?"

"Na. Just wanted to talk to him. Got into it with Jake Turner and the bikers last night.

Messing with those guys could get him killed."

"Ya, someday he'll learn that the hard way."

"If you see him, tell him to give me a call."

"OK but you never know when he'll turn up."

Chapter 9

At 12:30 P.M., it was time to go get the doctor and head over to Millie's restaurant for the "Big Welcome Party' Something Clancy was not looking forward to. He knew that in a town like MacAbee it was important to have a first rate Doctor. Old Doc Hamilton was in his seventies and wanted to retire. The new doctor was only twenty-eight years old. She could be here a long time.

It was with great reluctance that Clancy found himself in front of medical clinic of greater MacAbee, as pre Mayor Toms orders. There were still quite a few people in the waiting room even though the sign said the clinic was closing at 12:30 P.M.

"Hi, Sheriff." Called out a young boy.

"Hi yourself, Bobby." The sheriff called back. "Staying out of trouble. " As he said this, he rested his hand on the butt of his gun, a jester young Bobby didn't miss.

"Yes sir, not me. I'm a good guy," Said nine year old Bobby Clayton.

Bobby's mother was an old friend of Clancy's, since high school. She smiled up at Clancy and said. "Good to see you Clancy, don't see much of you around anymore."

"Duty calls, Sandy. Say hello to Ralph for me though."

"I will."

Clancy stuck his head in the window that separated the waiting room from the offices.

"Hi Jean, I thought were going to close early today."

"I thought so to. Now it looks like I'll be here all day."

Out of the corner of his eye, Clancy saw a tall willowy auburn haired woman talking to the Mayors wife, Agnes.

"Hi Mrs. Thomas. How are you today," Said Clancy.

"Why Clancy, we were just talking about you. Come and say hello to Doctor Whitmore."

Doctor Whitmore! Clancy was thunderstruck. Doctor Whitmore was beautiful.

Clancy Jameson Ryan, who is never at a loss for words, was speechless.

"It's good to finally meet you, Sheriff Ryan, she said as she extended her hand.

Clancy took her hand but didn't say anything. Dr. Whitmore stood there for a moment, and then said, "Sheriff Ryan."

The sheriff as if coming out of a daze finally said, "Sorry, I got kind of lost there."

"Does this happen often," she said.

"Not in a long while."

Rebecca Whitmore looked up into the eyes of the High Sheriff and almost blushed. Clancy held her hand and Rebecca didn't pull it away. Neither said a word.

Mrs. Thomas finally broke the silence. "We should be going if we're going to the party."

With the spell broken Clancy said, "Right. Can you leave with all these people still here?"

"Dr Hamilton says none of them are sick, just curious."

'Your coming here is a pretty big deal to a lot of the town folk."

"Like a prize hog, right Jean."

Jean gave Rebecca the evil eye and went back to work, leaving Clancy even more confused then ever.

"Did I miss something? He said.

"Not really. Jean and I were just comparing country life to big city misconceptions.

"OK, who won," laughed Clancy.

"Jean did. I've been here two hours and she already hates me."

"Not true," called Jean from the other room "I hated you before you got here."

Both women broke into laughter. Clancy tried to get the joke but soon gave up.

"We should go if we're going to get there on time," said Clancy.

"What's the rush," said Mrs. Thomas "Let them sweat a little."

Mayor Toms was the duly elected mayor of MacAbee, but the true force of nature in town was Agnes Thomas and everybody knew it.

Dr. Hamilton walked over and said "Good afternoon Sheriff. We should be ready to go in ten minutes or so. Just about enough time to make Toms sweat, right Agnes?"

"Perfect," said Agnes Dr. Hamilton excused himself and went to talk to Jean. Before Clancy knew it, the waiting room was empty of people and the doors were locked.

"So Clancy, ready to go," said the old doc.

"Not really Doc. I tried to talk Mike into going fishing with me but he said no."

"I'll go," said Rebecca, "This surly wasn't my idea."

All Clancy could do was stare at the new doctor.

"Now that would be perfect," said Agnes "Maybe we'll all go. Wouldn't that drive Toms nuts."

"Let's go," said the doc "Jean will lock up."

Chapter 10

The original Millie's was the typical downtown soda shop, set right next to the Old Arcade Theater. A clean place where kids could hang out after a Friday night movie and not have to worry about anything. There were ten small booths and a counter where Millie Stefano waited tables while her husband Nick did the cooking. Most nights, Nick Jr. was the busboy and dishwasher. After Nick went off to college a long line of MacAbee high school boys filled in at the grill.

Clancy Ryan and Mike Billings both had taken a turn at the sink.

In 1985, fresh out of college with a degree in business Nick Jr. persuaded his parents to mortgage the grill and their house to buy three acres of land at the south end of the MacAbee business distract to build the Stefano Supper Club and Banquet Hall. It was an over night sensation. From the moment they opened their doors, Stefano's was the place to go. Everything was first rate. During the weekday it served as the place to go for any type of business lunch or meeting. Friday night was for after the football games. Saturday was date night, with couples of all ages coming out for a nice diner and music. Nick always brought in a Jazz combo to play on Saturday nights so people could slow dance just like in the old days. Sundays, after church, Stefano's had brunch buffet that brought people in from all over the county, and even though the sign outside said Stefano's, the place will always be known as Millie's.

Today the banquet hall was decorated for the big welcome. There was a raised dais for the dignitaries, with a podium for speeches and tables for the guests.

The menu for today was fried chicken with sweet corn, followed by apple pie and coffee. The whole affair was the work of the Ladies Auxiliary. Whose chairwomen, Agnes Thomas, had strong armed the local businesses into 'donating' the needed funds. Everything was perfect as Mrs. Thomas saw it.

As Dr. Whitmore and Sheriff Ryan entered the hall they both cringed.

"Will you look at this," sighed Rebecca.

Hey, don't knock it," Said Clancy. "It's not every grown woman that gets to be the prom queen."

Rebecca punched Clancy in the arm and said, "Is it to late to run."

"Probably," said Clancy. "But if you want to try, I'll hold them off till you're gone."

"Tempting, but I think I'll have to take one for the team, besides how bad could it be."

"You're about to find out," Said Clancy pointing across the room.

Rebecca looked to where Clancy was pointing to see Mayor Toms practically running across the floor with the largest bouquet of roses she'd ever seen.

"Your court awaits you. Your Majesty," said Clancy as he stepped out of range of another punch.

"Hello, Dr. Whitmore, so nice to see you," beamed Mayor Toms, "And thank you for bringing her, Clancy."

"No problem Mr. Mayor. What time should I be back here to pick her up?"

Rebecca looked up at Clancy and said, "You're not staying."

"Of course he's staying, said the mayor. "Mrs. Thomas wouldn't here of him leaving."

"Look, I've got a lot of things to do today."

Rebecca gave him her best puppy dog eyes and said, "Please stay."

Clancy felt his knees go weak unable to speak.

"I don't know anyone here, please."

Clancy finally found his voice and said, "Dr. we've just met."

"I know but please."

"Alice, I'm going to be 10-8 at Millie's for awhile."

"I told you she was cute," Came back the return.

All Clancy could do was hang his head, When he looked up he saw that Rebecca was a shade of crimson Clancy had never seen on a women before.

I'm sorry Dr. Whitmore," He said in his most sincere voice. "There seems to be a conspiracy afoot to hook us up."

"I kind of got that impression by the way everybody kept telling me what a great guy you are."

"I'm not so great. I'm 34 years old and still not married; this gives my mother and her cronies something to fill their time."

"You don't share their ideals about marriage."

Clancy had just enough smarts left to know a loaded question when he heard one.

"I'm not against marriage, If someone came along that could be my best friend first and then a partner for life, I'd all for it.'

"We should sit,' was all she said.

Chapter 11

"On behave of the Ladies Auxiliary, I'd like to welcome all of you to today's festivities," began the mayor. "And I'd like to officially welcome Dr. Rebecca Whitmore to our little piece of heaven."

There was a loud round of applause. You could almost see Rebecca sliding down in he chair.

"Stand up Dr., take a bow."

Rebecca managed to rise about three inches out of her seat before setting back down. From her perch on the dais, she was able to look around the room at all the people she'd have to get to know real soon. The door to the hall opened and a deputy sheriff came in looking around until he spotted Clancy. The deputy made his way over to where the sheriff was sitting, whispered something in his ear that made the sheriff's face go sour. Sheriff Ryan stood up, walked over to where Dr. Hamilton was sitting, spoke to him where as both men stood and walked towards the rear door. Just before they got to the door, Clancy turned to the deputy. He pointed the Rebecca and said something to him. The deputy stopped in his tracks and remained in the hall.

It was at this point that Rebecca thought she heard her name being called. "Dr. Whitmore, Dr. Whitmore," said the mayor. "Would you like to say a few words?""

Damn," thought Rebecca.

Chapter 12

An hour later, Clancy and Dr. Hamilton were standing out on route 5 about five miles southeast of town, on the bridge that overlooked Puckett creek They were watching as two of the counties EMT's worked there way down to where a body had been found.

"Can you see who it is," asked Clancy.

"Not yet," called back the EMT.

"What do you think, Sheriff?" asked Dr. Hamilton.

"I don't think he jumped," said Clancy.

"We should be treating this as a crime scene."

"I agree. Have the guys back off for now. I want to do an evidence search first."

The EMT's, who were scaling down a steep incline, stopped and stared at the Sheriff. As they were considering their next move a brown minivan pulled up across the road from where they were standing. Clancy was surprised to see Dr. Whitmore, dressed in jeans and work boots, get out of the van and walk over to them.

"What are you doing here, "asked Clancy?

"I called the station trying to find you. Alice told me you had a D.B. out here."

"D.B.?"

"A dead body. I thought I could help."

"How are you going to help, guys dead."

Rebecca gave Clancy a hard look and said," Sheriff, every death of unknown origin should be treated as a crime scene. I thought that part of the reason I was brought down here was because of my training as a

Medical examiner. I have extensive training in forensic pathology and cause of death."

Clancy looked over at Dr. Hamilton, who shrugged and said, "That was a big part of it. I don't intend to run for coroner next time and Dr. Whitmore has all the nesseary qualifications for the job."

"Ok," said Clancy, "How do you want to proceed."

"First rule is to start with the body. Then work you're way away from it. Where's the body"

Both Dr. Hamilton and Sheriff Ryan pointed over the railing.

"It's almost sixty feet down to the creek," said Clancy.

Rebecca looked over the railing, down to where the EMT's were standing.

"How did anyone find him down there?"

"This is a local fishing hole. Two kids found him." Said Clancy, "Scared the crap out of them."

"How do we get down there?"

"We climb."

Fifteen minutes Clancy and Rebecca had finally climbed down to the river bed where the EMT's were waiting.

"Did either of you touch anything?" asked Rebecca. I is him him him him him.

Both men looked at Clancy as if to say, "Who's this."

"Well, did you," snapped Clancy.

"No. You said stop, we stopped."

"Good, let's take a look. Keep your eyes open for anything that's out of place.

Who knows what we'll find."

Just before they stared down the hillside, Rebecca pulled a huge case from the back of her van. Clancy, always the gentleman, offered to carry it for her. That turned out to be a big mistake. It must have weighed fifty pounds.

Rebecca opened the case and took out what looked like a very expensive digital camera. She then walked a ten foot circle around the body, which was lying face down, taking pictures every foot or so until she had a complete set from each point on the circle.

"Ok, let's turn him over on to his back," said Rebecca.

Clancy motioned for the EMT's to help her.

Stop, you guys got latex."

"You mean gloves."

"Yes, gloves," said Rebecca.

"Sure."

"Then put them on. Sheriff, could you get me a pair from the top drawer on the left."

"Sure," said Clancy.

Now that everyone was properly dressed, The EMT's slowly turned the body onto his back. Sticking out of his ribcage was the handle of a huge hunting knife.

"Shit, shit," said Clancy. That's Jake Turner. I had him in jail last night."

"I guess we can call this a suspicious death now," said Rebecca.

Clancy ignored her as he walked away.

"County one to dispatch."

"Go ahead Sheriff."

"Alice, get a hold of Mike Billings Tell him I'll need an arrest warrant for William Johnson as a person of interest in the death of Jake Turner."

"Oh my God," came the reply.

"Today, Alice."

"Aren't you jumping the gun here Sheriff?" asked Rebecca.

"I hope so," said Clancy. "I've known Will Johnson since kindergarten and that' his knife. He got locked up with Turner in our jail last night. He got into a fight with our deceased friend here out at Rollie's and was nowhere to be found after court.'

Rebecca continued to take pictures until she had every possible angle "There's blood spatter over here Doctor," said one of the EMT's.

Rebecca took a ruler out of her kit, laid it down next to the blood and took even more photos. She then swabbed the blood with a cue tip and put that in a small brown envelope.

"Sheriff," called down one of the deputies on the bridge. "We found blood up on the road and what looks like skid marks. Could be a bike went down."

"Secure the area but don't touch anything," The Sheriff called back up.

"That's a possibility Sheriff, look here," said Rebecca.

The back of Turners jeans had been scraped away, leaving a bright red gash that could only been road rash.

"I think we're done here," said Rebecca. "You can transport him to the coroner's office."

Both of the EMT's looked at each other then a Clancy.

"Coroners Office?"

"We don't have a coroner's office," said Clancy. "The last murder in this county was five years before I was born."

"Well where do you take the bodies?"

"Mostly to Micah Tolson's funeral Home,.

"Do they have a cooler there?"

"Yes and they have a room there where they prepare the bodies for the funerals. We can take him there."

"Good, Ok, guys, he's all yours."

Chapter 13

Clancy headed back to his office. He had to see about the warrant and he wanted to talk to Mike Billings before he went after Will Johnson.

Dr. Whitmore and Dr Hamilton had followed the EMT's to the funeral home to begin the autopsy and collect any more evidence.

Clancy parked his truck in his usual spot and headed for Mike's office, which was just across from the Sheriffs department. Before Clancy could enter Mike's office, Alice called to him form the dispatch office.

"He's not back yet. I had a hell of a time tracking him down. He's still with the Judge and will be back pretty soon."

"That's fine Alice. Call me when he gets back. I'm going over to the funeral home."

On his way over to Tolson's, Clancy saw Thom Billings getting into his truck outside of the hardware store. When he honked his horn to say high, Thom looked at Clancy, got in his truck and drove off without a word.

"Strange," thought Clancy. He noticed some fresh damage on the front bumper of Thom's brand new truck. Clancy made a mental note to ask Thom about that at a later date.

Pulling into Tolson's parking lot, Clancy was a little pissed to see three of the bikers sitting on their bikes.

"How the hell did word get out so fast," thought Clancy.

As Clancy parked his truck all tree of the men got off their bikes and walked towards him.

"Afternoon boys," He said. "Something I can do for you."

"Word is you got Jake in there."

"I can only tell you what I know. Ay about 1:30 this afternoon, Jake Turner was found out on route 4. I'm sorry boys, but he's dead."

All tree of the men looked down at their feet. These were hard looking men from years of living the biker life, but at that moment they looked lost. Finally the one who did the talking said,

"How'd it happen?"

It appears he dumped his bike."

"No way, "said the man. "Where's the bike?"

"Sorry, that's all I can tell you right now," said Clancy.

"What."

"You can do me a favor. I'll need to talk to Jake's wife. I'd appreciate it if you could tell her to come in to see me."

"What about."

"Sorry again, but that's police business. I assume she's next of kin."

Clancy turned and walked away, leaving the bikes standing alone in the lot. The last thing he heard as he closed and locked the door was.

"Jimmy's not gonna like this Sheriff."

"Now that's the truth," he said out loud as he closed the door behind him.

"What's the truth?"

Clancy turned to see Dr. Whitmore coming down the hall.

"Three of Jake's buddies are outside asking questions. One of them said that Jimmy, Jakes brother, is not going to like it. That as you would say is an understatement."

"So, you know these guys."

"Oh yea, these guys have been a pox in this county ever since they got here.

Jimmy's in prison because of me and now Jake is murdered, possibly by one of my best friends. This could get ugly real fast."

"How can this Jimmy be trouble for Jimmy if he's in prison?"

He's due to be paroled next month. This should insure an early release. He'll be here in time for the funeral."

"You've had trouble with him before I take it."

"Oh yea, I'm the one who put him in prison. He's going to take this real personal.

"What happened?"

"About two years ago, Willie, Mike and I were out to the state park fishing. On the way home, we stopped at Rollie's, your typical road house. Rollie's used to be a decent place until the Turner brothers and their gang turned up. They'd only been in town for awhile and didn't know us. I was in the men's room when it started. Jake picked a fight with Will and Jimmy went after Mike. No reason, just having their kind of fun. Willie's a brawler het took care Jake in no time. Mike's not a fighter. He was trying to get out of the bar. Jimmy was going to get him anyway. I stepped in between them, told Jimmy to back off.. Jimmy threw a punch at me and I pretty much beat him to a pulp. Then I arrested them all.

You should have seen their eyes when I pulled out my badge and my gun. We searched their car and found two unregistered handguns and a half pound of weed.

Jimmy was out on parole even back then, so he took the fall. Now we got this. I don't think there's going to be trouble, I know there will be."

"Didn't you say it was Jake and Willie that got into the fight last night?"

"Yea, so how's the autopsy going?"

"Well, cause of death was definitely the Knife wound. It went through the lung, into the left ventricle. He bled out in a hurry, possibly before he went over the bridge."

"Not much chance he fell on the knife as he was dumping his bike."

"Now that would make it too easy."

"And since we didn't find the bike, we have to assume that there was another person involved."

"Dr. Hamilton is finishing up. Do want to see him."

"No, I'll let the pros do their job. I'll read the report later."

Micah Tolson poked his head out of his office and said, "Clancy, Alice is on the phone for you."

"Hello Alice," said Clancy. "What have you got for me?"

It wasn't Alice but Mike Billings on the phone.

"Not much Clancy. I went to Judge Pennybrook to get the warrant and the old fool called Old Horace. Old Horace said he'd bring Willie in Monday morning, so the judge left it at that. No warrant."

"Jeez, the man is wanted for questioning in a capital murder case and he judge gives him a three-day pass," Yelled Clancy.

"The judge thought our evidence was highly circumstantial."

"I wasn't looking for an indictment; I only wanted to talk to him."

"We'll just have to wait for Monday. Come on Clancy, its Willie. You don't think he would kill a man, do you?"

"I don't know what to think but I have to do my job. Let me talk to Alice."

"Hello Sheriff," said Alice."

"I want you to call every deputy on duty and tell them to arrest Will Johnson on site."

"Would this be this legal Sheriff. What would be the charge?"

"I don't know. Put him in protective custody."

"Ok, but if I go to jail, I'm taking you down with me."

"Deal, make the calls."

"Good bye, Sheriff."

"Good bye Alice."

After he's hung up the phone, he turned to Dr. Whitmore and said, "What's left to do here?"

"I'll check with Dr. Hamilton before I go home but I think we got all we're going to get. The blood samples will be sent to Springfield and the knife will be printed and filed as evidence"

Rebecca paused looked up at Clancy and said; "So I guess I'll go home."

"Where are you staying?" asked Clancy.

"I'm at the Wilson's B&B."

"B&B stands for bed and breakfast not bed and dinner, would you like to go to dinner first."

Rebecca gave Clancy a sly smile and said, 'Bowing to the will of the Ladies Auxiliary."

"Very funny, I didn't get anything to eat at the luncheon today and you're not going to get anything at the B&B. It'll give us a chance to talk about the case."

"Ok, but let me go back to the B&B.. I'd like to clean up first, if you don't mind."

"Great, I'll pick you up at 6:30."

Chapter 14

At ten minutes after six o'clock, Clancy Ryan was standing in front of his mirror acting like a school girl getting ready for the prom. He had put on his best suit and tie, to formal. This wasn't a date he told himself. Finally, he settled on a new pair of jeans and a pull over shirt. Just the casual look he wanted.

Five blocks away, Rebecca was having the same problem. After she had showered and put on a low cut, skin tight cocktail dress. As soon as she looked in the mirror, she knew that it would never do. Talk about sending the wrong message.

After looking at all the clothes she had brought to town, she finally pulled on a pair of jeans and a tee shirt. At the last minute she grabbed her favorite corduroy jacket.

"Much better, she said.

Clancy always kept his county truck at his house. He was always getting calls at all hours of the night and it made things easier. Tonight, no police truck, no gun, police anything. He called the dispatch office to tell them where he'd be but left word not to call him unless there was an emergency.

When Clancy's father was alive, they'd shared a passion for old cars. As a boy, Clancy would help his father tinker with the long line of heaps his father brought home.

They'd fix them up and sell them in order to buy the next heap. When Clancy's dad died; he had left several cars in various stages of repair. Over the years, Clancy had spent many a Sunday afternoon working on the last three cars he and his father had bought. He felt he owed it to his father to finish them.

Tonight, he'd take out the '65 Cheval Malibu SS Convertible. Cherry red with a white canvas top and custom white leather bucket seats. The car had best of show style and he knew it.

Chapter 15

His second car was a '72 Hurst Olds 442 that still needed paint and a little more chroming before it would be finished. The transmission needed to be rebuilt but it was close.

Back in the corner of his garage under a tarp was a car Clancy never thought he'd finish. It was the pride of his father and Clancy never felt he could do it justice.

The frame and all the parts needed to restore the car were there but He'd never even worked on it. It was a 1963 Corvette convertible California fuel injected roadster, one of only 3000 made. His father loved the car and was going to rebuild it from the ground up. He died before he could get to it, leaving Clancy to agonize over it.

With the SS's top tucked neatly under the custom red rear boot, the car was washed, waxed and ready to go. It was the kind of car that they didn't make anymore and it was looking good tonight.

Rebecca was sitting out on the front porch when Clancy pulled into the driveway of the B&B. when Rebecca stood up, Clancy almost chocked. She was just beautiful, no doubt about it. Mrs. Wilson was beaming with a big smile.

"Why Clancy Ryan, don't you look handsome tonight."

"Why, thank you Mrs. Wilson. It's always good to see a member of the Ladies Auxiliary," said Clancy as he gave Rebecca a wink.

"Now I gave Dr. Whitmore a key to the front door so don't worry about a curfew tonight."

"That's great Mrs. Wilson but we're running off to Vegas to get married so we won't be back till Monday morning."

"That's very funny Clancy Ryan. I'm sure your mother will get a big kick out of that one, "she said with w twinkle in her eye.

Clancy bent down and gave Mrs. Wilson a kiss on the cheek, which made her swoon a bit.

"You can assure the Ladies Auxiliary that the High Sheriff of MacAbee county is not out to corrupt the morals of out towns newest doctor.

Rebecca was so busy trying not to laugh out loud that she was startled when Clancy took her elbow and led her of the porch. She turned to say good night to Mrs. Wilson who was still glowing. Mrs. Wilson gave a short wave and said," Have a good time tonight," and hurried inside.

"She'll be on the phone to my mother before I can get the car started."

Rebecca turned towards the car in question and stopped dead in her tracks.

"This is yours?" she asked.

"Yep, you like it."

"A '65 SS convert, what's not to like. Those aren't stock seats and I've never seen a boot like that before. It looks fully restored. Bet it's got the 283 with a four barrel carb.

"Yea," said Clancy a little stunned. "It's pretty much a stock motor with a few modifications. It was the last car my father and I worked on before he passed. He always sold what we fixed but I couldn't sell this one."

"It's beautiful. How could you ever sell it? It must mean so much to you."

"It doses and you're right, I'll never sell it. Someday I'll give it away."

"Maybe you could keep it for a son."

"That would be alright with me, let's go."

"Where are we going, Sheriff?'

"Do you think you could call me Clancy? I'd like that, if you don't mind."

"Only if you'll call me Rebecca."

"It's a deal."

"Great," she said as she jumped into the drives seat and said," Where to."

Clancy stood there for a moment then threw her the keys and got in on the passenger side.

"There are not a lot of choices in a small town like this," said Clancy, "And there In lays the dilemma. We have three choices tonight. None of which appeal to me for very different reasons. We could go down to the Grill but that will be full of High school kids, it being Saturday Night. Another place we could go would be out on the Interstate. There are a lot of nice restaurants out there. Trouble is their almost all connected to motels and since I made that promise to Mrs. Wilson, it wouldn't be a good idea to be seen out there."

"Yes, perception is always more important then reality."

"Plus, with the whole department out looking for Will, I don't want to be thirty miles away."

"What's the third choice?"

"We could go back to Millie's."

"That seems ok."

"Yea it is but like you said perception is greater the reality."

"I don't understand."

"It's Saturday night. Everybody in town will have found their way to Millie's. My mother is meeting the mayor, his wife and The Billings there for dinner. I was asked, but declined. You know what they're going to think."

"I think it will be fine. What's the worst that could happen anyway? Maybe a few tongues will wag, so what."

"You realize that by now the whole Ladies Aux knows that we're out tonight. They will all stand up and cheer as we walk in."

"That would sure make it fun,' Rebecca said with a mischievous look in her eye.

After they had driven awhile, Clancy broke the silence by saying, "You're not what I expected."

"What did you expect?"

"I didn't have a clue, but I'm glad you're here. I'm somewhat surprised by how comfortable I feel around you. It feels as if I've known you longer that one day."

'Yea, I feel it to but I'm still an old fashion girl, Clancy Ryan. There could be something here and I hope you'll have the patience to wait till its right."

"Let's get some dinner."

Chapter 15

The parking lot at Millie's was packed.

"I told you," said Clancy.

"Wow, where do I park."

"Take it right up to the front door. When I was a kid I used to work at the grill downtown,. Now Nick treats me like Royalty."

Rebecca pulled the SS up to the front door where a young man about 17 years old wearing a bright red coat jumped out of his seat and opened Rebecca's door.

"Hi Sheriff, you really gonna let me park the SS for you," he said.

"Dr. Whitmore, I'd like you to meet Mickey Stefano, son of Nick and Grandson of Millie. Mickey is a real stand up guy, who would know better then to go joy riding the Sheriff's favorite car, right Mickey."

"Right Sheriff, park it right next to the door," Said Mickey. "Glad to meet you Dr. Whitmore, Welcome to MacAbee."

"It's good to meet you also, Mickey," said Rebecca. "Take good care of her, it's a classic."

"I know doc. I've been in love with this car ever since he finished it. When are you gonna get to the other cars, Sheriff?"

"What other cars?" asked Rebecca.

"The Sheriff's got a whole garage full of classic car just waiting to be restored. Tell her about the Corvette."

"Corvette, you got a Corvette."

"Half a Corvette really. It's in pieces"

"What year, what engine?"

"It's a '63 covetable 327, Californian fuelie."

Rebecca's mouth dropped. "You got a porcupine in your garage."

"Yea, but like I said, It's in pieces. How do you know so much about cars anyway?"

"I got three brothers and two uncles that would race anything that would run. Every one of them a gear head. I took my drivers test in a '69 RS." She said as they walked through the doors to the restaurant.

At the wait stand Nick Stefano stood as if he was waiting for them.

"Clancy, welcome, how are you tonight."

"I'm good Nick. I'd like to introduce you to Dr, Rebecca Whitmore, Our new doctor."

"Great honors Dr. We are so glad you are here."

"Thank you Mr. Stefano."

"You call me Nick. It's a small town and we're all family here.

"In that case it's Rebecca."

"I got a table all ready for you by the fireplace, come.'

"Nick, how'd you know we were coming tonight?"

"You're momma called, told me you were going out with the beautiful new doctor. Where ease would you come but to Millie's."

Clancy looked at Rebecca, who was smiling, and said, "So it begins."

Chapter 16

As they walked through the crowded restaurant, Clancy felt as if every eye in the room was on them. He greeted people as they went, stopped to chat wherever nescerie. Just when he thought they'd make to a table he heard the unmistakable voice of Mayor Toms.

"Clancy, oh Clancy, over here, come over here."

Clancy turned towards the mayor and his party, which included his mother but not to his surprise Mike and Bea Billings.

Clancy leaned into Rebecca and said, "Now the real fun beings."

Rebecca thought about hitting him again but thought it to playful for the watching crowd.instead she said, "Come on, let's say hi. We'll be fine."

Mayor was on his feet well before Clancy and Rebecca made it to their table.

"What a day, what a day. Dr. Hamilton has been telling us about the 'you know' the mayor leaned close and said in a whisper, the murder. Imagine, Willie Johnson killing that biker."

Clancy gave Dr. Hamilton a sideways glance and said, "I'd sure like to know where you heard that bit of information."

Dr. Hamilton gave Clancy a hurtful look and said, "Not from me, I assure you."

"I have my own sources. After all, I am the mayor; I need to be kept in the loop."

"Fine," said Clancy. "But we don't know who killed Jake Turner and I don't want to hear you talking out loud about it in public."

"Loose lips sink ships, right Clancy," Said the mayor.

"Right, by the way, where Mike and Bea. I thought they'd be here tonight."

"Mike called and said something came up over at the courthouse and he'd be here later."

"Do you know what it was?" asked Clancy.
"No, but here they are now. Ask him yourself."
Sure enough, Mike and Bea Billings were making their way across the room.

"We need to talk, Clancy," was all he said.

"Ok, but could we get something to eat first, I'm starving."

"Why don't you come to Sunday dinner tomorrow afternoon and we can lay it all out. Bring Dr. Whitmore."

"Oh yes do,' Said Bea, who was making her own introductions. "I would love to have you come by. We're to become great friends."

"Sure, I'd love to, "said Rebecca.

"Excuse me Sheriff, Do I have to shoot someone to get your attention," came a voice Clancy had know all his life.

"I'm sorry mom. It's been a rough day," Said Clancy.

"No reason to be rude." She said as she turned towards Rebecca. "I'm Elizabeth Ryan, you can call me Beth. We met this morning."

"Yes, I came in to get my grandsons records,' She said. "He's going to play football this fall up in Naperville"Rebecca looked back at Clancy.

"Jack's my nephew; he's my sisters' kid. Jack Johnson's his name."

Rebecca got it right away but the look on Clancy's face told her to wait until they were alone.

"We're going to sit now,' said Clancy. "And eat."

"Before you go you should know that Mary Beth Turner never showed up back at the farm after court," said Mike.

"Do they know this at the station?"

"Yea, I put it out before I came over here, that's what kept us."

"Why wasn't I notified?"

"We tried. We called your car and your house. Finally one of the deputies saw the SS pulling into Millie's. Funny thing was, he said that a woman was driving it. You never let me drive the SS," Mike said with a sad look on his face.

Clancy stared at Mike with an "I'm gonna kill you" look. Everyone at the table laughed, while Rebecca blushed. Clancy growled, "We're gonna sit now. I'll see you later, Mr. Billings."

Clancy turned to Rebecca, took her by the elbow and walked away.

Chapter 17

"I'm so sorry about that," said Clancy. "They mean well enough.

"I know. Makes a girl feel right at home."

Clancy spotted Nick waiting patently at their table.

"Sorry Nick, but you know how they are.'

"Not a problem Clancy, Their all good people. Let me buy you both a drink, what'll it be Rebecca?"

"Do you have Blue Moon On tap."

Nick gave Clancy a look that Rebecca didn't understand and then said, "Yes we do, we just got it in. The usual for you Sheriff."

"Sure,' Said Clancy.

Nick disappeared and in a flash a waiter reappeared with two Blue Moons.

"What?" said Clancy when Rebecca gave him a look. "I developed a taste for it when I was in D.C. Around here its Bud and More Bud and Bud Light. When I came back here I talked Nick into stocking it."

They talked about nothing and were just about to order when a loud crash came from the bar, followed by what sounded like a fight.

"Now what?" said Clancy as he looked over his shoulder.

"You'd better go,' was all she said.

"Would you please order me the Penne chicken pasta and a side salad with blue cheese."

Rebecca laughed out loud.

"What did I say?"

"We have the same drink and the same dinner. Maybe we should make the announcement right here."

"Very funny, don't you start on me too."

Another loud crash came from the bar.

"Go."

Clancy headed towards the bar at the same time Mike and Nick did. The bar at Millie's was small, not meant to be a hangout, only a place for people to wait for a table. Still People did come only to drink. On a Saturday night, Millie's was crowded and so was the bar.

When Clancy got into the bar area, he saw Thom Billings being held down by one of the bartenders and Mike Todd, One of his deputies.

"What happened, Mike?"

"We were just having a beer before going home when Thom came in. He's drunk and Joey wouldn't serve him. He told him to go sleep it off."

"That's right Sheriff," Said Joey. "Mr. Nick says we don't serve anyone if their drunk."

"He's right Clancy," said Nick. "This isn't Rollie's."

"Go on Mike."

"Well, Thom here gets mad and starts to yell. All I did was put my hand on his shoulder and asked him to calm down."

"That's right Sheriff,' Said Joey, "Nice and easy."

"He told me to 'mind my fuging business', he pushed me into the crowd. That's when he picked up the beer mug and busted the mirror. I'll bet you heard that."

"We all heard that," said Nick.

Mike Billings turned to Nick and said, "I'll take care of everything. Just send me the bill. I'll make it right, Ok"

"It's not just the money Mike," said Nick. "We work real hard to make a nice place for families to come and enjoy a good time. I can't have this in my place."

"I know and I'm so sorry," said Mike.

Clancy turned to his deputy and said, "Who are you here with, Mike."

"Jason, we were just having a beer after work."

"Don't worry, you're off duty. I want you and Jason to take Mr. Billings over to the the jail and let him sleep it off. Tell dispatch to call Old Horace. Tell him we got Thom. Can you do that for me?"

Turning to Nick, Clancy said, "Can we wait until Monday to talk about charges."

"If Mike makes good on the damages, I don't think there will be a complaint."

"That's up to you, but I got him for assaulting my deputy so I'll hold him on that."

"Your not serous are you," said Mike.

"This is the third time today I've seen Thom acting out of the ordinary. I'd like to know what's going on here. I'd like to know where he was today about noon and how his truck got busted up."

"Probably hit a fence or a tree."

"Or maybe a motorcycle out on route 4"

"Wait a minute. Watch what you're saying here," Said Mike who was getting a little hot.

"I don't know anything. Until I know what's what, I got to look at everybody and everything, That's my job and I'm gonna do it. The last time I looked it was your job to, or am I wrong."

"You're not going to put this on my uncle just to save Will .

"Damn, Mike. You should know better then to say that. I'm oing to do this by the book and let it fall where it falls, and that's that."

Clancy stormed off in the general direction of his dinner guest. It only took him a few steps to notice that there was no sound in the room. When he looked around he saw that everybody in the room was looking at him. Clancy thought he should say something but decided against it. He held up his hands and walked back to his table. There he found Rebecca patiently sipping a fresh Blue Moon.

"You sure know how to show a girl a good time, Ryan, She said.

"I'm sorry Rebecca. I didn't mean to be gone so long. At least the food isn't here yet."

"The food came and went twenty minutes ago. Mr. Stefano came by and took it away. He said he'd bring fresh plates as soon as you were done with Mr. Billings."

"Man I'm gonna start eating the table cloth if I don't get some food soon."

When Rebecca smiled at Clancy, he felt a little light headed. He blamed it on lack of food.

"You and Mr. Billings seemed to be arguing," She said."

"That was Mike's uncle that busted up the bar. I sort of said that the damage to Thom's truck could have been made by hitting a motorcycle."

"I assume that he didn't like that very much."

"Not much at all," Clancy said. "He accused me of trying to put the blame on Thom in order to save Willie."

"We're you?"

"Maybe, I just can see Willie killing anyone. It's not in his nature."

"Tell me something?" she asked. "Your mother said that your nephew's last name was Johnson. Is there any connection?"

Clancy let out a long sigh and said, "Yea, father and son. Will was married to my sister for about Twelve minutes. I think they got divorced at the reception."

"Oh no," Rebecca said.

"Yea, it's a big time conflict of interest."

"We're going to have to be very careful on this one."

"One hundred percent by the book."

About this time the waiter came by with fresh plates of food along with two more

Blue Moons.

"God, that smells good," said Clancy.

"Mr. Nick said to tell you that the dinner is on the house tonight, just don't forget to

say good-by before you leave."

"Please tell Nick that it's not right for a elected official of the county to except things for free."

"Ok, I'll tell him, but he's not gonna be happy.

Clancy was so busy eating that he didn't notice Nick Stefano standing at the table.

"Sheriff Ryan," said Nick.

Clancy stopped eating in mid fork.

"Are we not friends."

"Of course we are."

"So you would honor me by accepting my hospitability, No"

"Nick, it's just not tight for you to give away favors to elected officials. What would the mayor think?"

"Do you really think the mayor pays for his dinners whenever he's here?" said Nick. "Please, for the beautiful young Doctor, Ok."

"Fine," said Clancy. "For the doctor, as long as I can eat in peace."

Chapter 18

The next morning, Clancy was sitting at his kitchen table reading about him in the morning paper. Most of what he was reading, he already knew. What he didn't know was that he and the good doctor were now an item. The article went on to say how they're romantic dinner was interrupted by the drunken escapades of Thomas Billings, uncle of the sitting county attorney.

"One day," said Clancy. "One day was all it took."

He was about to get another cup of coffee when his two year old golden, Gator began to growl.

"What is it boy."

Gator was growling at the door, wanting to go out.

Clancy looked out his window. His garage door was up. He knew he put it down last night.

"What now," he thought.

He slipped out the side door and went around to the window. There was definitely someone in the garage. Clancy walked in and said "Don't move," in his best cops voice.

Dr. Rebecca Whitmore jumped about four feet in the air, spun around and yelled at Clancy.

"Clancy Ryan, you scared the hell out of me."

"What are you doing here?"

"I was out jogging and I wanted to see the 'vette."

"You could've knocked on the door. I'm a cop, remember. People get shot around here for sneaking into other peoples garages."

"I'm sorry, I guess it was one of those spur of the moment things."

"How did you know where I live".

"Who else has a truck that has Sherff written on the side of it."

'Yea, well, OK. Let me get my heart rate back to normal. Do you want a cup of coffee?"

"Sure, that would be nice."

When Rebecca stepped out into the sunlight, Clancy almost passed out. She was wearing a very tight pair of running shorts and a wife beater tee shirt cut four inches above her navel and not much else'

"You're staring again Sheriff."

"Jesus, Rebecca, you go by the Baptist Retirement Home dressed like that, you're gonna kill somebody."

"Like what."

"You know, half naked."

"I'm not naked, I was out running. Maybe I should wear an overcoat and a pair of combat boots?"

"Around here, that might not be a bad idea."

"I guess I still have a lot to learn about small town living."

Clancy was still staring at her when she said, "Can I see the car?"

"Sure, it's in the back."

Clancy slowly rolled back the tarp that covered what would have been his father's last project. Under the tarp was the body of the 'vette, with all the parts laid out In order. Ever part was accounted for. All of the numbers matched.

"The only thing that needs replacing is the canvas. Should look good as new after it's painted."

"Are you ever going to finish it?"

"Yea, maybe some day. It would take about a year just to get ready for paint. "

"How would you start?"

"You start with the suspension, then the brakes. Electric, drive train and then the body. Last, the engine. That would take a lot of hours.

"It sounds so simple."

"If it was, it would be done. Let's get that cup of coffee," said Clancy as he rolled the tarp back over the car.

"What about the Olds."

"It's ready for paint, but I'm in no hurry on that one."

"Why."

"Jack, my nephew, has done a lot of work on it. Use to come over on Saturdays when he still lived in town. I thought I'd give it to him when he graduates for high school. He's only a sophomore right now, so I have some time. I'm afraid that if I finished it to early, I'd be temped to give it to him I think his mother would hate me forever if I did."

"So you should build the "vette.""

"Maybe, if I find the time. It was my father and me on the SS, then Jack on the Olds. I'm not very good at working by myself."

"What if I helped you?" said Rebecca.

Clancy didn't know weather to laugh or not, but she was dead serious.

"You'd do that, give up you're time to help on the "vette.""

"Sure. I'm going to be here. So why not?"

"Let me think about. We still got this other problem to clear up, but it's possible. Come on, let's get that coffee."

As Clancy closed the garage door, he saw his next door neighbor standing and staring at them.

"Good morning, Mrs. Lynch," said Clancy. "Have you met our new Doctor?"

Rebecca walked over and extended her hand. "Good morning Mrs. Lynch. I'm Dr. Whitmore, It's good to meat you."

At the mention of 'New Doctor,' Clancy thought that Abigail Lynch, age 85 was going to faint.

"Good morning." she said in a matter of fact manor. Then she added, "Are you Catholic."

"Why, yes I am."

"I thought so." And Mrs. Abigail Lynch turned and walked down her drive way to a waiting car full of little blue haired ladies.

"What, I, what did I do?"

"Baptist," was all Clancy said.

Rebecca laughed out loud and when Clancy joined in they got hysterical.

"It gets worse. You just met one of the founding our members of the Ladies Auxiliary.

They meat every Sunday after Church to decide on how to fix all the problems we have here in MacAbee. Add that to what was in the paper and you should make a lively topic of conversation."

"What was in the paper?" asked Rebecca not laughing anymore.

"Come on inside and take a look."

Once inside, Clancy handed her the paper.

"Oh no, they'll think I spent the night."

"I don't think so. I saw Mrs. Wilson last night when I dropped you off and you must have seen her this morning, right."

"Yea she made breakfast this morning."

"So I think you'll be safe on that account. They'll only get you for parading around half naked."

"I am not half naked, these are my running clothes.'

"Rebecca, listen to me. As the towns new doctor you have to be careful what you do. People around here will hold you to a higher standard them you were used to in Chicago. You are a truly beautiful women and people will notice what you do.

I'm totally screwed here, aren't I?"

"Not really, I'll talk to my mother. Between her and Mrs. Wilson you'll be fine, though I'd invest in some sweats if I was you." Clancy was making a fresh pot of coffee, when the phone rang.

"Sheriff Ryan."

"Clancy, it's me."

"Where the hell are you Willie?"

"I can't say right now."

"Can't or won't."

"Look, I didn't kill that asshole. I was with someone all day yesterday. We left right after court."

"Where did you go."

We were at the Holiday Express out on I-75."

"Who's's we."

"I can't tell you that."

"Willie, are you with Mary Beth Turner."

"How the hell did you know that?"

"Great. Now I've got I motive."

"It's not like that, Clancy. She was going to leave him and he found out. That's at the fight was about."

"You got to come in. I can't do anything for you if you're running."

"I can't. Old Horace wants me to stay away until he clears this all up."

"Old Horace told Judge Pennybrook he'd bring you in Monday morning. If he conned the judge to help you get out of town the judge is going to blow his top. If you don't come in, I'm going to have to come after you. I've got no choice."

"Well at lest I know where we stand," And he hung up.

"Shit," said Clancy. "Shit."

"Was that Willie Johnson," asked Rebecca.

"Yea, hang on a minute."

Clancy took the phone and punched in a code that gives you where the call came from.

"Chicago, He's at a 312 area code. I should have guessed. Give me a minute, I got to call Mike"

Mike billings answered after several rings.

"Hello."

"Hi Mike, its Clancy."

"Hello." Ha said rather coldly.

"Just had a call form Willie."

"Really," he said a little more interested know.

"He's in Chicago and he's got Mary Beth Turner with him."

"You got to be kidding me."

"I wish I was. What's more, it was Old Horace who got him out of town."

"You think he's going to run."

"He said they spent the whole day out at the Holiday Express by I-75. He said that he didn't do it."

"And you're buying it."

"Well, I'm sure going to check it out first."

"Ok, are you still going to come to dinner today?"

"Let me ask Rebecca first." Clancy turned to Rebecca and said.

"Do you still want to go to Mike and Bea's for dinner this afternoon?"

"Sure, sounds like fun."

"The doctor is there right now? Did she spend the night?"

"No, she did not spend the night."

Clancy covered the phone and said to Rebecca,

"Should I tell him you're half naked though?"

Rebecca hit him square in the chest and mouthed the words, "I'm gonna kill you."

"We'll be there about 3:30 or 4 o'clock, ok"

"Great, I'll tell Bea dinner at 6 o'clock."

Clancy hung up the phone rubbing his chest.

"We're going to have to work on this hitting thing of yours."

"You deserved it." She said with a sly smile.

"Yea, probably," Said Clancy. "But it sure would have made Mike nuts, wouldn't it."

"That would have been an evil thing to do, Clancy Ryan,"

"Yes it would," Clancy said with a smile.

They drank their coffee and talked about cars, just small talk. Finally Clancy said, "I've got to talk to Thom Billings this morning. Then I'm going out to the Holiday Express to check on Willies story. Why don't I pick you up around three today?"

"Why don't you pick me up after you talk to Mr. Billings? I could ride out with you to the motel."

"Why would you want to do that?" Clancy asked. Even though he had asked her why, he was kind of happy she'd wanted to come along. In less then twenty-four hours, this woman had really turned Clancy's head. He didn't know what to make of her yet.

"I got nothing to do and maybe I could help. If there's any evidence to collect I'm your girl. Besides, on the way we can talk about our "Vette project."

"I'm not ready to commit to a 'Vette project just yet, but if you want to come along, I'd be happy to have you.

'Happy to have you,' what was Clancy thinking. He was turning into a fourteen year old boy again.

Rebecca was also thinking, 'I'm your girl.' "Good lord what signal did that send."

"Why don't I pick you up in an hour?"

"Great. Should I change or is this ok?" she said with a smirk

Clancy gave her a look but didn't say anything.

Chapter 19

Clancy parked his SUV In his spot and went to his office first. There he booted up his computer and logged into the Police data base. He pulled up the search engine for phone numbers and typed in the number of the phone Willie had used. It showed a pay phone at Roosevelt and Halsted. Next he pulled up Map Quest and saw that it was on the south side near Cook County Hospital. Now that was interesting. He'd have to ask Rebecca about that later.

He next opened the state prisons website and looked up Statesville prison in Joliet, IL. When he typed in James T. Turner he didn't much like what he got back.

Turner, James T. In transit pending release MacAbee, IL.

"That's just great," Though Clancy. He reached for the phone.

"Statesville Prison, Joliet."

"This is Sheriff Ryan from MacAbee County, IL I need to talk to whoever id in charge today."

"Just a minute," came a rather chilly reply.

"Hello, this is deputy warden Siles, how can I help you Sheriff Ryan."

"Warden Siles, you're releasing James Turner early."

"Let me look. Yes, we are. He'll be driven from here to Ma-cAbee at 8 o'clock tomorrow morning."

"Why so early."

"Apparently his brother just died."

"It was yesterday at 3 o'clock. That seems pretty fast to me. Doesn't it take longer then 24 hours to process an early release like this."

"It does, but with his brother's death and his parole date coming up, the warden thought it would be ok to send him down."

"I'd prefer that you hold him until at least Friday if you could."

"You don't understand. He's officially paroled."

"That's going to complicate things," Clancy said as he hung up.

Clancy sat thinking about Jimmy Turners return to town. With Jimmy back in MacAbee, things could get violent real fast. Word had probably gotten around town that they were looking for Willie in connection with Jake's Murder. Who knew what Jimmy would do?

Clancy called Mike and told him about this new development. Mike was not happy to hear this.

"Not much we can do about it today is there," said Clancy.

"I don't know. Maybe I can call Springfield tomarrow and talk to the parole board.'

"By the time you get a hold of some one from the parole board, he'll be here."

"We can talk about it this afternoon when you come over."

"Ok, I'm going out to the Holiday Express to check it out. Maybe Willie was telling the truth."

"I hope so, if only for Jack's sake."

After Clancy hung up, he called his chief deputy, Tom Thomas Jr. "Tom, at roll call tomorrow I need you to make sure every man knows that Jimmy Turner will be in town at 8 o'clock in the morning."

"Oh man, when did they do that?"

"Warden up at Statesville felt sorry for him on account of his brother dying. I need you to get the word to al the men, ok."

"Will do, Sheriff. Some of the guys are coming over to watch the Rams Game. I'll get the ball rolling right away."

"Great."

Clancy looked at the clock and knew he had to hurry if he was going to talk to Thom Billings before he had to pick up Rebecca. He went down into the lockup and got the keys to the cell. Thom Billings was sitting up, but didn't look so good.

"Good morning Thom. Looks like you had a rough night?" Clancy asked.

"Screw you." was the reply.

"Are you going to tell me what that was all about last night?"

"No."

"Can you tell me about the damage to your truck?"

"No."

"I saw you arguing with Old Horace and Neil Johnson yesterday. What was that all about?"

"We were talking about football."

"Ok, if you change your mind and want to talk, then just tell the deputy and he'll know where to find me."

"When do I get out of here?"

"You'll see the judge in the morning. I'm sure he'll let you go home then."

Chapter 20

Clancy pulled up in front of the B&B just as Rebecca was coming out the door.

Once again, Clancy was taken by how beautiful she was. She was dressed in jeans and a sweater, much more conservatively then this morning. It seemed to Clancy that she dressed down on purpose. Still, she was stunning.

"So you think this will pass inspection," she said as she got in the truck. Clancy could here the edge in her voice.

"Are you mad at me?"

"Should I be?" Once again an edge of coldness had crept into her voice.

"I hope not. What's wrong, you seemed ok when you left my house."

"I don't know. On the run home I got to thinking about why I came here and everything seemed wrong somehow."

"I don't understand, what could be wrong," said Clancy. "This is a great town and we need you here."

"I know, it's just…," her voice trailed off.

There was a long silence that made Clancy uneasy. He didn't want to pry into her life if she didn't want him to.

"You can tell me if you want. I'm a pretty good listener."

"Something happened in Chicago. Something that made me want to get out of the city. I thought I could hide from what happened by coming here, but now I've become the center of world. I don't think I can do this."

"It will all pass soon enough. Just let it die down before you beat yourself up over being a celebrity."

"I came here on a lie. I lied to everyone. I even lied to myself."

They'd been driving for awhile when Clancy pulled the truck over to the side of the road. He looked at Rebecca with what she thought a strange expression and began to unbutton his shirt.

"What do you think you're doing, Sheriff Ryan."

Clancy didn't say a word until he'd pulled his shirt down off his shoulder exposing a large round scare.

"Do you know what this is, Dr. Whitmore."

"Oh Clancy, No one told me you'd been shot."

"I was standing in the middle of the road directing traffic in D.C. southwest. A bad accident was blocking most of the road and I was trying to get people to move along when I got hit. Came out of nowhere and we never found out who it was.

The doctor told me it was a high powered hunting rifle. The shot went clean through so no real damage. I came home to MacAbee to recover and never left. I quit the police department and had no idea what I was going to do."

"Why are you telling me this," asked Rebecca warily.

"I want you to know that you are not the only one hiding here."

"Do you know about what happened to me in Chicago?"

"Yea, I know."

"Why didn't you say something?"

"I figured it was your business and if you wanted to talk about it you'd do so in your own time."

"How did you find out?"

"Dr. Hamilton wouldn't tell Mayor Toms much about you, so he asked me to look into things. I was a little curious myself so did an internet search on the police network. I ran your name through the data base and all of the police reports

came up."

"So everybody in town knows the new doctor s afraid to go back to her big city job because she got the shit beat out of her." She was close to tears and Clancy knew he had to say something.

"Nobody knows."

"What, you said the mayor put you up t it."

"I don't work for the mayor, a thing that he can't remember most of the time. If Dr. Hamilton wouldn't tell him why should I. It's still your business."

"You didn't tell anyone," sniffed Rebecca.

"No, I buried it."

"Thank you. I guess you're as good as people say you are."

"No, I'm not. I know you're secret, you should know mine."

"No it's ok."

"You should know. When I got back to town, I was ashamed about the way I got shot. I didn't tell anyone about it, saying it was nothing and please let it go. They made me out to be this big home town hero because I never told anyone about the shooting.

Next thing I know everybody is telling me to run for sheriff. I knew I would never go back to D.C. and in need of a job, so I did it. Who would have thought I'd really get elected."

"So, what are we going to do?"

"I like my job and I've become good at it. I like living in a quite town like MacAbee.

What options do I have? I'm going to keep doing the job I was elected to do and I'll live with the rest of it. I can't tell you what to do but you'll always know you're not alone here."

Rebecca was quite for a long while, sitting there thinking about what she'd just heard.

"Pull over."

"What?"

"Stop the car."

Clancy pulled the truck to the side of the road but before he could ask what was wrong, Rebecca threw her arms around Clancy's neck and hugged him till it hurt.

He couldn't pull away even if he'd wanted to, which he didn't. After awhile she sat back and said, "Thank you for telling e. You've never told anyone any of this, have you?"

"How could I."

"What now."

"Neither of us set out to deceive anyone, we are who we are. We're the people who the town comes to when they need help. You're a doctor and I'm the law.

We both have jobs to do and I for one think we should do them. I'm not willing to give up what I got here and I hope you see it to."

Rebecca still had her arms around Clancy's neck. Clancy's hands had found Rebecca's hair. The look in her eyes was warm and inviting. Clancy was having a hard time breathing and his stomach was doing jumping jacks when a police siren went off.

Both Clancy and Rebecca jumped a mile. Clancy looked down to see if he'd bumped something as a county squad pulled up along side of them.

"Everything ok, Sheriff," Asked the deputy.

"Yea, we're fine," was all he said as he put the truck into gear and drove of. They drove in silence for awhile before Clancy said, "What was that?"

Rebecca blushed and said, "That was a little embarrassing. What will he say?"

"I didn't mean the deputy and he won't say a word."

"I'm sorry, Clancy. I was overwhelmed by your kindness and understanding. It's a little confusing to say the least. I've been here for two days and I'm already involved in a murder and been caught parking with the sheriff like a school girl. This was supposed to be a nice quite town. This is much to fast for me."

Clancy let it go, for now, but he was going to have to face what had just happened. He'd never felt what he was feeling right now for anyone before. To tell the truth, the High Sheriff was scared to death.

Chapter 21

The parking lot of the Holiday Express was crowded. Clancy parked the truck in the loading zone.

"Police business." He said. "You want to stay in the car or do you think it would be ok to be seen with me at a motel."

She hit him again.

"Again, Next time you hit me I'm gonna…."

"You're gonna what," she said. "If you deserve the hitting you got nothing to say.

Did you think that was funny?"

"Humor is the best defense against thinks that you're afraid to face."

"I'm coming in."

At the front desk, Clancy showed his badge and asked for the manager. A short, bald man stepped out from a side room behind the desk.

"Good morning Sheriff, What can I do for you," He said.

"I need to know if you or any of the hotel staff have seen either of these two people yesterday between 12 noon and say 5 o'clock," Clancy said as he passed the manger pictures of Will and Mary Beth.

"Sure, I've seen both of these people. They're here about once a week. I checked them in myself at a little after noon yesterday. As far as I know, they're still here." He checked the deck book and said, "No ones checked out yet."

"Can you open the room for me?"

"That's highly irregular Sheriff."

"I can get a warrant if I have, of course that would mean clearing the hotel of all the guests. But that's up to you. I'd have to go back to MacAbee and get the warrant. That would take an hour, all the while your guests standing around waiting for me to get back."

"Ok, I'll open the door," Said the little man." I hope there's no trouble."

The manager got his master key and told them to follow him. At the door Clancy took the key and said," Will, it's Clancy. I'm coming in. Stand back."

The room was a mess. The sheets were twisted and thrown all over the place. The tables were upside down and TV was on its face, down on the floor.

Rebecca pulled on a pair of rubber gloves and began to look around.

"Clancy, we got blood here," she said. "I didn't bring my kit. We're going to have to bring all this back to town."

She turned to the manager and said, "Do you have any large garbage bags."

"I'm sure we do," said the manager, who seemed to enjoy being involved in an ongoing police investigation. "Let me look."

He left but was back in a hurry with a box of plastic garbage bags, "Will these do?"

"Perfect," said Rebecca.

There was no sign of either Will Johnson or Mary Beth Turner.

"Gather up everything," said Rebecca. "We'll take it all back to town and analyze it there."

"Seal this room," Clancy told the manager. "Don't let anybody in and don't have anybody clean it. I'll let you know in a couple of days if we still need to come back."

"Not a problem Sheriff. I'm only to glad to help."

"Thank you," said Clancy.

Rebecca had two full bags of sheets, towels, pillow cases and wastebasket stuff.

They carried everything to the front desk. Clancy told her he'd get the truck and then help her with the bags.

Clancy drove around to the front of the building and pulled up to the door. As he stepping out of the truck he ran right into the Reverend C.S. Moony, Pastor of the First Baptist Church of MacAbee, his wife, three deacons and four members of the church choir.

"Why, good morning Sheriff. We didn't except to see you way out here."

Before Clancy could say a word Rebecca came out the door carrying one of the bags.

"Where should I put…" was all she got out before she froze at the sight of eight pairs of eyes, all staring at her. Not one person was talking. They were just looking at her as if she was standing there naked.

Reverend Moony, I'd like you to meet Dr. Rebecca Whitmore, our new town doctor." Clancy said as quick as he could, "Dr. Whitmore is lending her expertise to the Turner case."

Rebecca extended her hand and said, "I'm very glad to meet you, Reverend Moony."

"Yes, welcome to our town."

There was an awkward moment of silence before the Reverend said, "I understand you are a Catholic."

"Why, yes I…" was all she got out before the Reverend said, "Well, good day. I'm sure we'll see you around town Dr. Whitmore."

With that said, the Reverends entourage moved towards the adjoining restaurant, leaving Rebecca and Clancy standing alone in dead silence.

"Do they still stone people around here," said Rebecca..

"Na, we burn at the stake," Said Clancy.

They got into the truck but Clancy didn't start it right away.

Clancy finally looked at Rebecca with a smile and said, "We could be in Vegas by this time tomorrow if we drove all night."

Rebecca stared at Clancy for a long minute before she started to laugh. Pretty soon both of were laughing uncontrollable.

"Let's get out of here before we get into real trouble," Clancy said as he started the truck.

Chapter 22

When they finally got back to Macbee, they stopped at Thorsons so Rebecca could put the evidence in the cooler. After that Clancy dropped Rebecca at the B&B to change. Clancy went back to the Sheriff's office to make sure all their actions were properly logged in. He wrote a short report that added to the growing Turner case file. After that all he could do was closet his eyes and worry about what was beginning to be a truly strange event.

Chapter 23

At three o'clock Clancy drove over to the B&B and picked up Rebecca. Out on the front porch Mrs. Wilson waved at him.

"The doctors already left she said to meet you at the Billings"

At first Clancy was confused but the more he thought about it the more it made sense from Rebecca's point of view. She had too much Clancy for her first day in town.

As he drove over to Mike and Bea's, he tried to think how to handle seeing her there. Since he had no clue he decided to just wing it.

Bea open the door and said, " About time Ryan, we're about to give up on you."

As they walked into the house Clancy began to look around the room. There were more people there than he expected. He knew everyone there so he didn't need to make smalltalk. He was looking for her.

"She's in the kitchen." Said be.

"Who's in the kitchen," deadpanned Clancy.

"Clancy Ryan, I've known you since before kindergarten. Don't think for a minute you can fool me. Rebecca is in the kitchen."

"That transparent," said Clancy.

"Your entire life you've been an open book."

"Fine." He said as he headed towards the kitchen.

He stood in the door watching as Rebecca stirred the pot of something. She finally looked up and saw I'm standing there. Her face lit up with the most beautiful smile Clancy had ever seen. Bea, who was standing beside him elbow him in the ribs.

"What is with you women and your willingness to beat on me."

"Just comes naturally with you I guess," said Rebecca.

Bea tactfully retreated to the living room as Rebecca put down the spoon and walked up to Clancy. She put her arm around his neck as if they'd known each other for years.

" Sorry I didn't wait for you," she said. "I was feeling a little antsy just sitting around. I called Bea and told her I'd make a desert and here I am. Had to go to the market, but it's going to be good."

Clancy started to say something but Rebecca stopped.

"Let me finish before you say anything. I'd come here to hide, to get away. I needed to recharge. Today, in the truck before the deputy came", she paused for a long moment and then said, "I would have, in the truck, with you, I would have.

Later that thought scared me for a bit till I realize I can't spend my whole life walking on eggshells. I'm a grown woman, a Dr. of medicine I'm proud of that. So I decided that from this moment on I'm going to let things happen as they may. I'm going to be part of this town come hell or high water. I made the right decision coming here. I know that now.

There was another moment of silence were Clancy didn't know if he should speak when she said.

"And, I should tell you, Mr. Ryan, as for what happened today, I'm sort of mad that the deputy showed up when he did. I don't know what you want out of all this but I'm telling you this, if the whole town thinks that we're an item we shouldn't make them out as liars."

Clancy was again speechless.

"Well," she said.

"I, I I" he said.

Clancy stood at an moment in his life in a apex so to speak he knew his life was about to change. In 24 hours he'd gone from confirmed bachelor to hopelessly in love and he was apparently the last to know. He couldn't think of anything witty to say so we just reached down and pulled her to him and kissed her as passionately as he could.

"I think we have liftoff," came a voice Clancy knew all too well.

" Hey Mike perfect timing as usual."

"It's my house, besides the three of us have to talk. Now works for me."

It's Clancy looked back to Rebecca, she had a watery faraway look in her eyes.

"Can you give us a moment."

"Sure, come into my office I got to make a call about Jimmy Turners release."

"You know he's coming home tomorrow." Said Clancy.

"I heard. Going to make sure it's nice and all legal."

After Mike, left Clancy turned to Rebecca and said," I've never been very good at the relationship thing, it,s been a long time since I've felt anything for anyone, I got it for you. Once that deputy showed up all I could think of was this might have been my only chance. When you weren't at the B&B, I thought you were telling me to back off. I can't do that. We're both past the point where hiding what we feel is even possible. Do I want to see this thing through hell yes I'm never been in love, truly in love so I didn't know what it was like. I'm sure I would like to find out."

It was Rebecca's turned to pull Clancy to her. They held each other until Rebecca said, "You grew up here, but you left. I'm from Boston. You've lived in DC and Florida. I've lived a lot of places, but were here now. I'm not a big believer in coincidences. Sometimes things happen for a reason, and maybe, just maybe this is why. Still it's all so confusing. Falling into the arms of a man I just met is not really me. Yet here we are. What do we do?"

Clancy looked at her for a second and then said, "We have a lot of options, but I think what would be best for us, is to do nothing."

"Nothing, how can we do nothing."

"I don't mean nothing, nothing. I mean just be ourselves. Live our lives and let this thing take a natural course."

"I assume Vegas is out, so what do we do? I don't need a one and done relationship. What if we succumb to the moment and then find out we're not who we thought we were. I want to know you, really know you. Even the best relationships have to start as friends, and I so want to be your friend."

"I think I can guarantee that. So what, we pretend nothing is going on here?"

"Not at all. In fact I'd say we do the exact opposite. The more were together the better."

"Okay," said Rebecca." But what about our more immediate needs."

All Clancy could do was smile at that. It'd been a long time.

He finally said," well I think that Mike and Be might be a little put off if we ran out of here before dinner". This may Rebecca laughed out loud "Yeah, but since my morals already tarnished around here why not?"

"We need to talk to Mike. Them lead dinner. Okay"

"Okay."

Mike was still on the phone when they knocked on the door to his office. He waved them into the chairs and said" 1 min."

As they weighted their hands briefly brushed. As if by reflex Rebecca slipped her hand into Clancy's so their fingers intertwined. This little of them was not missed by the County attorney, who stopped what he was saying and started a to of them. He covered the mouth piece of the phone and said," I'm I missing something here."

Clancy laugh while Rebecca felt a bit of blood rush upper neck.

Mike ended the phone call and said they're looking at the two people holding hands

"All right, what's going on." Was all he said.

"What do you mean, Mike." Said Clancy

"Don't play dumb with me, you two, what?"

"We don't know what's going on," said Rebecca," it's still a mystery to us to."

"Clancy, I'm your best friend have been for more years than I remember."

"And," said Clancy.

Just then Bea stuck her head in the door and tried to begin talking. Her eyes focused on the intertwined hands and said nothing.

"Okay," she said." This is weird. You got some explaining to do Ryan."

" Okay look," said Clancy," have you ever met someone for the first time and felt

like you've known them forever."

Mike can Bea both said yes.

" That's all I can say, Rebecca is a special person. What can I say." said Clancy.

Bea began to smile," I had a feeling about you to. Oh and dinner is ready."

" Bea," said Rebecca," please don't make a big deal about this. It's hard enough for me being new here so could we keep this between us for now."

" Boy, are you asking a lot." Said Mike," this woman is to MacAbee what the Internet is to the world. An information superhighway.,

" Bea," said Rebecca.

" Biggest story of the year and you want me to just sit on it."

Was all Bea could say.

" Please." Said Rebecca almost begging..

" Okay, heck I've been trying to get this boy hooked up before years."

" Bea, gives five more minutes okay," said Mike

" Okay."

After Bea had left Clancy said," so how are things are going this Jimmy Turner."

" 8 AM tomorrow morning he's out."

" Great, there's nothing we can do about it?

" No, but that's not what I wanted to talk about. Dr. Hamilton called me this morning. Told me how you handled the crime scene and the autopsy. He was very impressed, Impressed enough to ask me to Appoint Rebecca as the official County medical examiner you take over the case from Dr. Hamilton and he'll remain as corner. What would you say to that?"

" Jeez, I thought things move slowly in small towns. I'd actually be happy to do it. I training for just this kind of thing." Said Rebecca.

" Fine," said Mike." You'll work as needed and you'll have Dr. Hamilton's old office at the County building. And by the way you also get paid."

" Really." Said Rebecca

" It's not a lot of money but we've all been pushing for a bigger budget, I think were going get it this time."

" Why's that?" asked Clancy, He'd been involved in many a budget war himself over the years.

" Well, there just may be a new business willing to build a factory in MacAbee County. They've been talking with Mayor Toms and old Horace."

" What kind of company?"

" Don't know yet. Commissioner Bigsby asked me to look into rezoning a parcel of land owned by old Horace just pass route 4near 17."

" Right next to the old Turner place right?" Asked Clancy.

" Yeah, coincidence right." Said Mike.

" Well I'll be look into that," Said Clancy.

" We should join the others." Said Mike as he rose from his chair.

Chapter 24

Dinnerr was going great. Everybody was laughing, telling stories, most about Clancy and Mike when they were younger. Clancy told one about Bea, and Bea told what about Clancy and they all laughed.

As dinner began to wind down Bea began to clear the dishes, Rebecca stood to help. Soon they were alone in the kitchen. Bea said to Rebecca, " it's been years since I've seen Clancy so relaxed. I'm amazed by all of this. But I'm happy form. He's a great guy and deserves a great gal."

" Am I reading something here?" asked Rebecca.

" Oh I'll admit to a huge crutch on Clancy Ryan, ever since high school."

" Did you ever date?"

" No, Clancy wasn't in the dater. He was a jock. He and Willie ran the school.

Mostly out of my league. Now Mike is the kind of guy you take over to meet you mother."

Both women were laughing when the phone rang.

" Hello," said Bea," yes he's here. Just a minute, it's for Clancy."

Clancy came to the phone and it didn't take long for him to lose his happy face.

" I got to go." He said after had hung up." Some of the dirt bags from Turners are

trying to take Jake's body. They want to have a Viking funeral out at the farm.

There over at Tolson's right now."

He looked at Rebecca and begin to say something but stopped.
" Look," he said "Can we get together later?"
" Of course, I'll either be here at the B&B. Call me when you get free."
" I will."
He thought about kissing her but didn't.

Chapter 25

After Clancy left, the party slow down. After coffee and Rebecca desert, most of the guests left.

Bea was washing the last of the dishes and Rebecca was wrapping a large piece of the desert she was hoping to give Clancy later that night, when the phone rang again.

" Hello" said Bea," oh hi toms. What. She looked at Rebecca, then looked quickly away.

" Yes, she still here. What, oh no. I'll tell her."

She hung up the phone, looked over at Rebecca and called for her husband.

" Mike, come here."

" What is it."

" I want you to drive Rebecca over to the to clinic, please."

"Why, what's happened?"

She turned to Rebecca and said

" Clancy's been stabbed."

Rebecca felt herself go light headed is the blood ran out of her.

" Is it bad." She stammered.

" They didn't say. Just for you to get over there fast."

Mike already had his keys and was heading out the door.

"Come on, I'll get us there in 2 min." he said.

On the drive over, Rebecca could hardly contain yourself. He had to be alright.

How could fate do this to her.

When they got to the clinic, have to deputies were there milling around.

" Where's Clancy." Asked Mike.

" Inside would Toms Junior." Came the reply Rebecca was nearly running at this point. She threw open the door to the examining room and saw the Sheriff Clancy had on, cut and bloody lying on the floor.

" Oh no." She said out loud.

" You're too late, he's gone." Said Toms Junior.

Rebecca pushed past Tom Junior almost knocking him to the floor. She ran into the examining room, and found it empty.

" I don't understand, where is he?" She cried.

"I told you he's gone." Said Tom Junior," he went home."

" Went home," she yelled." Went home. You said he was gone. I thought you meant he was gone, like dead."

" Naw, Clancy's fine. Just the Nick. It's the other guy you should go look at. We got him chained to a bed the next room."

Sure enough, one of the bikers was chained to the bed in the room B., Bleeding from his nose and mouth.

" This is going to need a few stitches, " She told him.

Chapter 26

20 min. later, Rebecca had finished with the biker Mike had left with one of the deputies who had brought Rebecca's rental van back. Rebecca cleaned up then left for the B&B. Her first thought was to go to Clancy's but she needed to clean up first.

Once in the room at the B&B Rebecca was able to calm down enough to consider calling Clancy. She looked at the phone, but didn't call. Instead she decided to just go over there and yell at him in person.

Chapter 27

Clancy had not gone home right away. He drove to Mike and Bea's looking for Rebecca. When he got there, Bea told him what Tom Junior had told her.

" Shit ,she's gonna think on dying something."

At about this time Mike came in and told him what had happened that the clinic.

" Toms a dead man." Clancy was feeling." That's just like him to play stupid like that."

Clancy called the clinic but got no answer. He then called the B&B. Mrs. Wilson said she hadn't seen Rebecca since that afternoon.

Clancy decided to drive out to the clinic, but found no one there, and didn't see you Rebecca's Van. Next you went by the B&B still no Van he drove around town a little bit more than finally one home.

Clancy parked his truck and went inside. He was about start washing up when the doorbell rang.

" Now what?" He said.

When he opened the door he was surprised to find Dr. Rebecca Whitmore. As Clancy started to open the door, Rebecca pushed past him with her hands on her hips and glared at him.

" What?" Was all he could think to say.

" Do you have any idea what that asshole deputy did to me tonight?" She fumed.

She was defiant and really pissed off.

" Yeah Mike told me, I'm so sorry."

" I thought you were dead."

Clancy. The change in her voice as a tear ran down her cheek. He moved across to her as fast as he could, put his arms around her and held her.

" Why would he do that?" She said stifling a wheeze." He laughed, he thought it was so funny. Why would he do that?"

" He wants my job. I'll bet you a dinner at Millie's, he talk to Carter, and Carter told all about seeing us out on the highway."

She was starting to calm down, still holding her head against Clancy's chest.

" What for God sakes is happened to me." She sounded very tired. Hell of a first couple of days. Is it always this way around here?"

" No," said Clancy," this is the slow season. Wait till football season, that's when the real fun starts.

Rebecca pushed away from Clancy and said," don't you make jokes, just don't."

" I'm sorry. Can I get you a drink of water."

" No. I need something a little stronger. What to you got?"

" I'm not a real big hard liquor guy, but I've got some beer and some California wine downstairs."

Clancy had been remodeling his basement for years until it was now very comfortable recreation room. It had a bar to one side next next to a pool table. At the far end was a sitting area with an overstuffed sofa and Ottomans. In front of the couch there was a state-of-the-art entertainment system. Big-screen, stereo system, and what looked like computer.

" Pretty fancy system Ryan, what's with the computer?"

" It's the heart of the system. It helps control everything, plus it loaded with hard drives so I can store all my music and movies. It also records off dish network or Sirius radio so I can watch things when I have time."

" Sounds expensive."

" Not really, been picking up a piece here and a piece there for almost 3 years.

" How does it work?"

Clancy handed her what looked like a small flat screen TV.

" Just hit the power button."

She did what told her and the whole thing just came a life.
"Wow."
" Now hit music."
She hit the music button, and a list of bands came up on the TV.
She selected a band and a list of albums came up. She picked the
album, and a list of songs appeared..
She selected a song and immediately started to play.
" That's really amazing Clancy."
" Yeah, it's a lot of fun."
Clancy had sat down on the side table with two glasses and an
open bottle of wine.
" I think this is a wine moment," he said.
 Rebecca had calm down playing with Clancy system. She sat
down on the sofa, put her feet up on the ottoman and sighed.
" This is really nice."
Clancy handed Rebecca glass of wine and said, " I'm so sorry your
first taste of MacAbee was so sour."
She looked at him with a coy kinda smile.
" Not at all," she said." I just might like it here."
Clancy sat down next to her, and took her hand. They sat there
holding hands.
After a while, Rebecca saetdown her glass and rolled in the Clan-
cy's lap. She put her arms around his neck and said,
" Yep, there's a lot to like around here."

$\mathcal{P}art\ 3$

"The Homecoming"

Clancy woke up early the next morning a little bit disorientated. He knew where he was, but something wasn't right. Where was Rebecca? Their lovemaking had been slow and tender, starting on the sofa downstairs, and ending up in bed upstairs. Now she was gone.

While Clancy laid there thinking, the smell of something cooking came racing up the stairs. Clancy smiled to himself thinking this could be alright, when Rebecca came through the door wearing one of his shirts, carrying a tray full of food.

"Hungry?" She asked

"Yes and I could use a little food to."

"Jerk." Was all she said as she sat down the tray and jumped into bed.

Clancy sat up just enough to pull Rebecca to him. He kissed the top of her head, then her neck.

"Are you going to let this food get cold?"

"I like cold bacon and eggs."

"No really, let's see now. I need to talk about something."

Clancy sat back, took his plate and began to eat.

"How did this happen, Clancy?"

"What you mean, this?" He said with a bit of a smirk, "I think it was the wine."

"Clancy I'm serious. Two day's is all it took for me to change the way I think

about everything."

"You're not having regrets are you?"

"Hell no, I'm still trying to uncurl my toes."

"What?

"Nothing. Look, Clancy," she took a long breath before she said," Downstairs while I was cooking, I got to thinking about everything. You know, what I wanted and all. I kept coming back to one thing and one thing only Clancy. I've falling in love with you. There I said it. It's a bit overwhelming to say something like that. It's a first for me.

If this is going to be just a fling, something is going to be over in a few days or a week, I can't stay here in MacAbee, and it would be too much to take."

She stopped talking, looked down at her plate, but pushed the food around with your fork. She finally looked up and said," Well say something."

Without any hesitation, Clancy grabbed Rebecca, kissed her and said,"Rebecca Whitmore, will you marry me?"

Rebecca was stunned speechless, flabbergasted. She had no idea what to say. She took a long deep breath and said, "You're serious, aren't you?"

"As a train wreck."

"That's insane."

"Anymore insane then telling a man you just met you're in love with him? More insane than sleeping with that that man after only two days. You said you couldn't handle it if it was just a fling. I guess this will clarify my intentions."

Rebecca was about to say something when the phone rang. Clancy let it ring, all the while staring at Rebecca.

"You going to get that?"

"Fine," he said." Hello."

"Good morning Clancy," came the voice of his mother.

"Hi mom, how are you?"

"There's a van parked in your driveway, and it's been all night."

Rebecca had a panicked look on her face.

"I also called over to the B&B. I was going to asked Dr. Whitmore to come to dinner. Mrs. Wilson said she never came home last night.

"Dr. Whitmore is missing?"

"And you have a van in your driveway?

"Better call the FBI mom."

"Just like your father, big joker."

"Mom, are you sitting down?"

"Yes."

"Nothing breakable in your hand?"

"No, what is all this foolishness?"

"This is going to sound a little crazy. Hell it sounds all crazy to me."

"Don't cuss."

"Yes ma'am."

"Please Clancy, what is it?"

"Rebecca is here with me now, she spend the night."

Rebecca threw up her hands, rollover on her stomach and put the pillow over her head.

"Clancy Ryan, what have you done?"

"Mother, what I have done is to ask Rebecca to marry me."

"What, I don't understand, marry you, you mean, marry you?"

"Marry me, as in be my wife."

"Good God. What, what did she say?"

I don't know yet. My busy body mother interrupted us at just the right moment."

Clancy nudged Rebecca in the ribs making her jump. She looked at him with eyes that meant kill.

All Clancy could say was." Well?"

Rebecca looked long and hard at Clancy. Clancy was beginning to worry she say no, when she smiled and said, "Yes Mr. Ryan I would be honored to be your wife."

"Mom, she said yes."

"Good God. Oh my, a, good God."

Clancy put his hand over the mouthpiece and said, "I think I finally made her speechless."

Finally Clancy's mother said," may I speak to her please?

"She wants to talk to you."

Rebecca's eyes got wide as she shook her head no, but Clancy pushed the phone at her.

"Hello Mrs. Ryan."

"Hello my dear, I have to say that I'm a little flabbergasted to say the least."

"I'm sorry ma'am, this is a surprise to me to."

"Are you sure?"

"Yes, I'm sure."

"Okay then, why don't you and Clancy come to dinner tonight?"

"I'd love to."

"Good, we'll be able to talk then. Are you going to call your parents? Oh and by the way, congratulations my dear."

Rebecca froze. My parents, oh God, she thought. "I guess I'll have to."

"Okay then, we'll see you tonight."

"Great, goodbye."

"Oh, Clancy," Rebecca said after she hung up the phone.

"My mother is going to pass away."

"Why?"

"Trust me, she is going to go nuts."

"What did my mother say?"

"She seems almost happy about it."

"More like relieved. I think she'd lost hope."

"We have a lot to talk about Mr. Ryan. As insane as this all is, it's going to get worse."

"So what. It's not about them. It's about the best thing that's ever happened to me, ever. What more do you want me to say? I love you to. No bullshit, just love."

She flew into his arms. There were going to be late to work this morning.

Chapter 28

It was after 10 AM before Clancy arrived at the courthouse. After parking his truck, he went looking for Deputy Thomas Thomas Junior. He found him in the call room doing his usual nothing.

"Hi Sheriff. What's new?"

Clancy grabbed him by his shirt and hauled him out of his seat. He pushed them back until his head hit the wall.

"You piece of shit. I ought to beat you to death right here."

"What, it was just a joke."

"A joke. You think it's funny to scare woman have to death?"

"What do you care? You trying to tap some of that?"

Clancy bald up fists with the intentions of breaking as much as Toms faces possible when Mike Billings and a deputy pulled Clancy off of Toms.

"Don't do it Clancy, "Mike said." There'll be hell to pay."

"I don't care, this piece of shit..."

"No Clancy, let it go."

Clancy shook free of Mike and the deputy, and leaned in to Toms.

"This isn't over. You stay away from the Dr. or I'll finished this. You got it, you

 got it?"

"We'll see real soon, won't we Sheriff?"

"What's that supposed to mean?"

"Nothing, nothing."

Toms picked himself up and stormed out.

"What did he mean by that?" Asked Clancy.

"I don't know."

'Clancy took a long breath. After he calmed down, he asked Mike,
"Is your uncle still here?"

"Yeah, he still downstairs."

"You want to talk to him with me?"

"Yeah, Old Horace has already called twice this morning. He wants
his foreman back."

"Tell him we'll trade him for Willie."

Thom Billings was sitting quietly in his cell eating whatever was
brought over from the diner. The looked up as Clancy and Mike opened
his cell door and walked in.

"So Thom, you want to tell me what's going on here?" Said Clancy.

"What do you mean Sheriff?" Tom said." Can't a guy get a little
shitfaced and blow off a little steam in this town anymore?"

"That's not I'm talking about Tom. I saw you arguing with old
Horace and Jacob Johnson. As soon as I pulled up, you took off."

"I have work to do. That punk Willie was supposed to get the
supplies we needed first thing Friday morning. Instead, he's nowhere
to be found. Found out he was in jail.

 Not a good way to start the day."

"What about your truck?"

"What about it?"

"I saw you in town Saturday about four o'clock. The whole front
end was busted up."

Thom turned to his nephew and said," What's this all about Mike.
What's this have to do with the bust up at Millie's?"

Mike looked over Clancy just shrugged.

"The guy Willie tangled with the other night wound up dead
sometime Friday afternoon right after they all got of jail. We found
signs of an accident out on route 4, but no vehicles. We found the body
at the bottom of the bridge over Pickets Creek and Thom, you been
acting pretty strange."

"No fucking way," he screamed.

"Okay," said Clancy." Tell me about the truck."

Toms said quietly thinking for a minute. Then he said," I don't know. I don't know what happened to the truck."

"Well, tell me what you do know. Start with where you were Friday."

"I can't."

"What you mean, you can't?" Asked Clancy.

"I can't."

"Look Thom," said Clancy." If we're going to clear this thing up, I think you'd better tell us what's going on."

"Okay, but this has to stay here with us, okay?"

"I wish I could promise that. Come on, tell us."

"I was with Diana Lang. We took her car. I didn't see my truck until I had to go to town, by then it was already busted up."

"Mickey Lang's wife?"

"Yeah."

"Uncle Thom, that's nuts."

"Mickey left her, went back to St. Louis and he ain't coming back."

"So why all the secrecy?" Asked Clancy.

"Diana didn't want people to think I was the reason he left."

"Were you?"

"Yeah, I guess so. But they were having problems long before I came along."

"Okay," said Clancy." Tell me about Millie's."

"What's to tell? I just let my temper get the best of me. Started drinking after I got back from town. Drank everything I could find. Once I'd ran out of booze I headed to town. I remember going to Millie's. I guess I cause a ruckus. Then I woke up here."

Thom sat quietly then said, "Is Nick going to press charges?"

"No, I took care of it." Said Mike." But it's going to cost you some money."

"I'm going to have to talk to Diana," said Clancy.

"Why?"

"I need to corroborate your story. I'm going to let you tell her, but I want to see her today."

"When can I go home?"

Clancy stood up and said," Hang on."

He walked the new the hallway and called out,"

"Deputy Walton could you come here."

Deputy Walton came into the hall and said," Yes Sheriff."

"Do you know where Mr. Billings' truck is?"

"Yes sir. We locked it in the maintenance garage."

"Good, take Deputy Street and fingerprint the truck's steering wheel and door handles inside and out. Take pictures of the damage to the front and lots of them."

"Okay, Sheriff, I'll get right on it, " Said the deputy.

"When you're done bring the truck here."

"Got it," the deputy said as he turned left."

"I told you, I had nothing to do with any accident."

"Well someone busted up your truck," said Clancy." If not you, then who? I'll need to talk to Diana Lang today, Thom. I'll let you know when you can come get your truck, okay."

"Fine."

"You're free to go."

Chapter 29

Clancy and Mike went back to Clancy's office after Thom Billings had left.

"What's the status on Jimmy Turner?" Asked Clancy.

"He'll be here at about noon. The state cops are driving him here to be released into our custody."

"Why's that?"

"I don't know. Seems a bit irregular to me."

"What are we supposed to with him?"

"I guess that's up to us. I'm seeing Judge Pennybrook later today, I'll ask him. My gut feeling is to just release him."

Clancy rolled his eyes, then said." We got one of Turners dirt bags locked up from last night. We could charge him with aggravated battery of a police officer."

"What would be the point of that?"

"We could make a deal with Turner. If he behaves himself, we don't press charges."

"I don't know about that Clancy. Doesn't sound very legal."

"Could be our little secret."

"I've got to go see Judge Pennybrook. I'll be back by 11 o'clock. I want to be here when Turner gets here."

Chapter 30

Just as Mike was leaving the phone rang. "Sheriff Ryan," was how Clancy always answer the phone and his office.

"Hi," came the voice of Rebecca Whitmore." You busy?"

"Not for you."

"Two things. First, the blood on the sheets at the motel was menstrual blood. Mrs. Turner must have had her period.

"I didn't know there was a difference."

"Men, of course there's a difference."

"You said two things."

"Yeah, how would you like to go to Boston with me?"

"Boston, to see your folks?"

"Yeah, once I tell them about us, my mother is going to go nuts."

"Should I be worried?"

"No, I'm hoping that once she meets you, things will go real good."

"What about your father?"

"Oh I don't think he's going to be a problem."

"Why's that?"

My father went to the University of Florida medical school. Big time Gators fan. I've lived with the whole 'Gator Nation' thing all my life."

"I like him already."

"Good, then you'll go?"

"Of course I'll go, we're going to have to see the Turner murder through first, okay?"

"Okay. We have a date at your mother's house for dinner tonight. Are you going to make that?"

"Maybe, got a lot of work to do yet. Either way I still want to see you tonight."

"Not a problem. Got to go, call me later."

"Will do."

"Oh, by the way, did I tell you I have Four brothers," She said as she hung up the phone.

Chapter 31

At about 11 o'clock, Clancy, Mike Billings and three of the County's biggest deputies, were standing outside waiting to for the state police to drop off Jimmy Turner.

They had radioed that they were about 10 miles out, so Clancy pulled the three deputies off the street had them stand by across the street. Some of the bikers had begun to congregate across from the jail. As long as things were peaceful he just let them be.

10 min. later the state car turned the corner and pulled into the courthouse parking lot. In the backseat sat James Turner.

"Sheriff Ryan," said a pretty good-sized state cop." I'm Sgt. Berry. Were here to remand James Turner into your custody."

A second officer help Turner out of the car. He was shackled, arms and legs.

Clancy turned to his deputies and said," Take Mr. Turner to the conference room. I'll be along soon."

As the deputies led Jimmy Turner inside, he turned a Clancy and said," Good morning Sheriff."

"Good morning to you Mr. Turner," said Clancy.

"We've got a lot to talk about Sheriff."

"And we'll get to that as soon as I can. Go with the deputies, I'll be along soon as we get done here."

As the deputies were leading Turner away Clancy said," I'm sorry about your brother Jim."

Turner looked back over her shoulder and said," That's nice of you to say Sheriff, but it doesn't change a thing, does it?"

"No I guess it doesn't."

After Turner and the deputies had gone inside, Clancy turned to the state police and asked." So Sgt., I guess we have some paperwork to take care."

"Just all the standard chain of custody forms. Shouldn't take more than a minute."

"Would you guys like some hot coffee?"

"It's all the same to you, I'd like to get this done and head out." He said this while looking at the growing number of bikers across street.

"Don't worry about that bunch. They're just here to collect the boss."

"Still, it's a two-hour drive back to Joliet and we really need to go."

"Okay, come on inside and we'll get this thing done."

After the state guys had left, Clancy waited another half hour before going to see Turner.

"What took you Sheriff?" Asked Turner.

"Paperwork, you know how it is, got to get it all right."

"They told me it was up to you when I get out of here. Is that right."

"Yep, could be today, could be in two weeks."

"Well what's it going to be?"

"I give it to you straight, James. I'm inclined to let you go today. Only thing is, I got to have your word that you and your friend will let Sheriff's Department handled the investigation. I know if it was my brother, I be looking the get into it."

"You got it all wrong Sheriff. I loved my brother, but this is Independence Day for me. That whole biker thing was his doing, not mine. I'm home because he was my big brother. With him gone, I'm free of it. Look, I have no desire to go back to prison. I'm done with all that."

"I wish I could believe you Jim. I think everybody deserves a second chance. But I got a little problem here. Most people around here think there's a meth lab somewhere in the County. And, most people think you and your brother the ones behind it. Turner said nothing to this.

"Look Sheriff, you have my word. I will not interfere with you or your deputies or the investigation in any way. I just want to bury my brother and get on with my life."

"I'm taking you at your word James, but remember, obstruction of justice is a parole violation."

"Oh I know you'd love the send me back to prison. I won't be any trouble."

"Okay then, you're free to go. One more thing, we got one of your guys, Bull Rigby, for assaulting an officer. I'm willing to let him go and drop all charges if you keep your word."

"Assaulting an officer?"

"Yeah, the asshole cut me, but I broke his nose, so I think we're even. Okay? "Yeah were good.

Chapter 32

As soon as Turner left, Mike Billings, who was listening the other side of the two-way glass, walked in and said,

"Do you believe him?"

"Not for a minute. The only thing he said I believed was he didn't want to go back to prison."

Through the open window they heard a cheer go up from outside.

"There he goes, the returning hero," said Mike as snidely as he could.

"What are we going to do?"

"Watch him like a hawk. I want to know his whereabouts 24/7."

One of the deputy stuck his head in the office door and said, "Mr. Turner would like another word with you Sheriff."

"Now what," said Clancy? Then after a minute he said," Okay I'll be right out."

Clancy walked out the side door and found the entire gang standing there waiting for.

"What else can I do for you, Mr. Turner?"

"I'd like to know when I can bury my brother."

I'll talk to the medical examiner tonight. Go make your arrangements and I'll see to the rest of it. That be okay with you?"

"That will be fine. I appreciate it. I'll call you tomorrow."

The roar of motorcycles drowned any and all sounds throughout the whole town.

"Going to see the medical examiner tonight?" Said Mike.

"Yeah, were having dinner at my mom's."

"Really? Dinner at Moms that sounds nice. All right Clancy, spill."

"Spill what?"

"Don't play me for stupid, tell me what's going on with you in the new Dr."

"Nothing, we're getting married."

To say that the look on Mike Billings face was a true mark of amazement would be the understatement of all understatements.

"What, what do you mean getting married?"

"What do you think I mean?"

"Whoa, hold the phone. You're kidding me right?"

"No."

"The Great American bachelor does not asked the girl to marry him in less than 48-hour's."

"Why not?"

"Bea is going to wet herself."

"Look Mike, you can't tell her that yet."

"Oh no, I can't keep a secret like this from Bea. If she finds out that I knew about this and didn't tell her, I'll be sleeping in the rose bushes, maybe under the rose bushes."

"Please, please keep this a secret. If it becomes absolutely necessary to tell her, you got to tell her to keep it a secret to."

"Right, Beatrice Billings does not know how to keep anything secret."

"Then you can't tell her. Look, she hasn't even told her parents yet."

"Boy I sure like to hear that conversation."

"I don't think I have too much to worry about. Her dad is an old Gator."

"Well that explains everything. How stupid of me." He said as he walked away shaking his head.

Chapter 33

Diana Lang called at two o'clock. She obviously did not want to talk to the Sheriff about her and Tom.

"If it gets around town that I spent the night with Tom, well you know."

"If you can corroborate Tom's whereabouts, then this is as far as it will go. If you lie to me, then you'll be an accessory to a capital crime and I can help you. So tell me the truth."

"I met Tom out at Rollie's, at about 7:30 Thursday night. We had a few drinks, then we left in my car at about 9:30. We went to my house where we spent the night. I dropped them off at the Johnson's farm about 10 o'clock the next morning."

"Did you see him at all the rest of that day?"

"No, <u>because</u> he was so drunk I didn't want anything to do with him."

"Okay, Diane. We're good here. I'll need to talk to you again if it becomes necessary."

Clancy went and stick his head in Mike's office.

"Diana Lang's story matches your uncle Tom's. But we still don't know where he was between 12 noon and 4:30 PM, when I saw him in town."

"If he was out at the farm all day, like he said, plenty of people should have seen him," Said Mike.

"I know I really don't like Mike for this. But I got to know about his truck. Look at this."

Deputy Walker had come back with about a dozen photos of the damage truck.

"See how uneven it all is. If it had hit a tree, it would have been more uniform."

"Was he able to get any usable prints?"

"Yeah, will run them but I'm guessing most of them will come back as Thom."

He thought for a moment and then said," We need to find the bike, then we could match up the damage. I wonder where it is."

Clancy looked up at the ceiling lost in thought and then said, "Hang on minute."

He walked down the hall to the call room where he found three deputies that had helped out earlier at the crime scene.

"I've got an assignment for you three."

" Good," said one of them." Get a little boring around here."

"I want the three of you to go out to where Route 4 crosses Puckets Creek. Look up the Creek in both directions and on both banks. Then looked up and down Route 4 in the bushes, in the woods if you have to. Do a real thorough job, cover everything."

"What are we looking for?"

"Jake Turner's Harley Flathead."

"I know that bike, bright red paint job with ape hanger handlebars."

"That's the one. If I'm right, it's going to be real close to the bridge or somewhere near Puckets Creek. Take two cars and keep in touch."

"Got it Sheriff."

As they got up and left, Clancy went back to Mike's office.

"Do you know anyone in the DA's office up in Chicago?"

"Yeah, why?"

"Maybe they can help us find Willie and Mary Beth."

"It's a big city."

"I know, but make a couple of calls. Maybe we can narrow it down a bit."

Clancy went back to his office and called over to the clinic.

"Dr.'s office, how can I help you?"

"Hi Jeannie, is Dr. Whitmore busy?"

"Not really, let me get her"

A few seconds later Rebecca came to the phone.

"Can't leave me alone for a minute can you, Ryan?"

"Why should I? Get used to It. Got a question for you."

"Okay, shoot."

"The phone call we got from Willie yesterday came from a pay phone near Roosevelt and Halsted. I was wondering if you know where that is."

"Yeah, that's real close to where I used to live. It's right in the middle of the UIC campus."

"Anything else about that area."

"Cook County hospital."

"That's where..."

"Yes," She snapped, cutting short.

"You volunteered," He finished.

"Sorry. Still little touchy about that."

"Hospital, interesting. Was the blood volume more or less than you'd expected?"

"More, but not unusual. If I was to guess, pending further tests, we might be looking at in early term miscarriage."

"Really? Maybe an abortion?"

"Yeah, that's possible."

"Thanks, that's just what I needed."

"What time are you done today?"

"About five I guess."

"Can you pick me up here at the clinic."

"Sure."

"See you then, by."

Chapter 34

Back in Mike's office, Clancy related what Rebecca had told.

"What if we send your friends in the DA's office a resent mug shot of Willie and Mary Beth? Could he get some of them over to Cook County hospital's emergency room?"

"The find out if Mary Beth was a patient there?"

"Yep."

"Give me a good set of pictures and I'll make the call."

Chapter 35

At about two o'clock the call came in. The dispatcher stuck her head In Clancy's door and said, "The guys up on Puckett Creek found the bike," she said.

"Great," said Clancy as he reached for his radio." County one to 14."

"14 here, go ahead Sheriff."

"Where are you, exactly?"

"About a mile north of the bridge on the West Bank."

"Good, stay there and don't touch a thing."

"It's pretty busted up boss and their some blood."

"Okay, I'm on my way. Alice, tell Mike what's going on." Said Clancy as he reached for the phone.

"Dr.'s office, can help you?" Came the answer after he dialed the number.

"It's me again Jean. Is the Dr. in?"

"You know, I'm beginning to suspect there something going on between you two."

"Whatever do you mean?" Said the Sheriff is deadpanned as he could." Is she there?"

"Just a minute."

When Rebecca came to the phone, she said," Why is Jean looking at me like that?"

"I think she thinks that there something going on between us."

"So what, why would I care who knows."

"Fine with me, but listen. My deputies found Turners motorcycle out by Puckett Creek. There are some blood can you get away?"

"Hang on. Jean, canceled this one and give this one to Dr. Hamil-

ton. See if you can reschedule this one for later?"
"I'll be ready when you get here," she said.
"Okay, I'm on my way."
Clancy made it to the clinic in about 10 min. Rebecca was waiting outside. She threw her two suitcases in the back in hopped in. She was wearing overalls, a raincoat and her work boots.
"You look like you've lived here for 30 years."
"Just trying to blend in."
They were barely out of town when Rebecca slipped her hand into Clancy's. His first thought was a warm one.
"This going to take a while till I'm used to this," Clancy said giving her hand a small squeeze.
"Don't take too long," she laughed.
"Would you like to drive down the St. Louis on Sunday, Maybe do a little shopping?"
"Shopping, for what?"
"On a little, shoes, maybe some new electronics, Engagement rings."
"You want to buy me an engagement ring?"
"Sure, why not?"
"I don't know, I hadn't really thought about it."
"I was going hold off, but you said you didn't care who knew."
"I don't, sure why not, we could spend the whole day."
"Good."
"There's one more thing you might be will to help me with."
"Anything."
"I need a place to live. The B&B is nice, but it's not a home is it?"
"No it's not."
"I think I need something a little more permanent."
"You could move in with me."
"I thought about that, but I think it may be too soon for that. I need a place of my own, for now okay."
"Yeah, that's fine. I guess I was thinking about this morning and how much I like you being there."
"Two homes doesn't have to mean two beds. I'm sure will spend most of our free time together."
"I sure hope so. It's not like we know much about each other yet."

"Plenty of time for that."
Clancy smiled as he said," the rest of our lives."

Chapter 36

At the bridge Clancy phone Deputy Stone waiting for them.

"It's all about a mile upstream. You can get about three quarters of the way back by truck the rest is walking."

" Lead the way." Said Clancy At the three-quarter mile point Deputy Brown was waiting.

Down the path take the right back to the creek. Look here before you go back. We delete got three sets of motorcycle tracks. Two are the same. The one that's different matches the bike at the bottom."

"So two bikes in, two riders, one bike out still two riders." Said Clancy.

"That's the way I see it. Look at these two, they're the same. Ones deeper than the other. Two riders make extra weight."

". Good work John." Clancy said as he gave Brown a congratulatory pat on the shoulder.

"Rebecca, can your digital camera get the depth of the tire tracks."

"I can to you one better." She said as she pulled one of her cases out of the truck.

"How about a plaster cast."

"Oh man, I love you." Said Clancy before he could stop himself.

Both deputies look at each other. Then at Clancy, then they looked at Rebecca, who had her head buried in her case. When they look back at the Sheriff, he was staring bullets at them. Neither of them said a word.

"One of you stay with the doctor the other show me to the bike. When you've finished here come down and will work the bike."

" I'll stay." Said Stone.

"Good said Clancy, "then you're with me Brown."

The bike was lying on its side have buried under branches and dirt, like someone wasn't really trying to hide. It was turned on its side and was pretty mangled.

"How many pictures did you take?" Asked Clancy.

"Two packs of 12", said Stein"Every angle we thought of"

"Good, did anybody touched the bike"

"No sir, we both kept at least 10 feet away."

"Good."

"Here comes the doc."

Clancy turned and saw Rebecca struggling down the side of the hill. With the cases he went over and took them both from he.

"Where Stone?'

"I left them there just to watch the molds.'

"Bikes are over here, Stein said they stayed at least 10 feet away.'

"Okay let me get some shots with the digital, then we can move the branches.'

Rebecca walked a circle around the bike, much like before.

Deputy Stein asked," why take extra pictures."

"High resolution, Pluse two eyes are better than one."

After all the pictures were taken, the deputies under Rebecca's is guidance, began to remove the covering. Each step of the way Rebecca took more pictures. When they finally uncovered the whole bike it didn't look drivable.

"You think they drove this thing here. Looks way too broken."

"Sure does.' Said Brown,' maybe they towed it."

" No look at this," said Rebecca.

She was holding two legs of tree limbs, each about the size of a baseball bat.

"The use this to busted up. The headlights are broken but the glasses still on the ground." Ground

"Why do you think they did that." Said Stein.

"So no one could drive it out of here.' Said Brown.

"Yeah, that way if someone did find it they couldn't take it away from here." Said Clancy, "Where's the blood?"

"Mostly on the tank in the handlebars, but we found some over near the water, right there."

Clancy looked where Brown was pointing and saw a small amount of blood.

Rebecca swabbed the area with the Q-tip and took more pictures than she placed the leaves that the blood was on in evidence bags.

"Okay guys.' I think we're done here. Let's get the plaster castings. I want this bike in the maintenance yard today. Call the Township garage and have them bring the flatbed out here."

"How long have you been a deputy Hank."

"Six years Clancy, you hired me."

"Good work today, all of you. There may be an opening for a shift supervisor. Put in for. I think you get what I'm looking for."

"Sure Sheriff thanks."

Back in Clancy's truck Rebecca said," I heard what you said to Deputy Brown. It was good work. He was very observant."

"Yeah he's a good man I've had I have to send someone to the state for training.

He would be my first choice."

"Clancy?"

"Yeah."

"If the bikers hid Turner's bike in the woods then we may be looking at an in-house killer"

"Yeah, and there's at least two of them. I'm going to have to talk to Jimmy about all this, but that can wait. About tonight?"

"Don't worry, I'll be fine. I think I heard a sigh of relief in your mother's voice."

"Very funny, but not all that untrue."

"I've got to go back to the clinic and process these blood samples. Why don't you pick me up at 5 o'clock?"

"Don't you want to clean up first?"

"Yeah, but I can do that at your house. That upstairs shower is huge. Big enough for two don't you think?"

Clancy gave a small shiver and said"I suppose it is.".

Chapter 37

Clancy sister, Letty opened the door as Clancy Rebecca were walking up the drive. They had walked over from Clancy's house to work off some of the energy from their "shower".'

Letty was tall, thin and very pretty. Same color hair as Clancy, same bright green eyes. Rebecca thought they could be twins.

Clancy step forward and hugged his sister.

". I didn't know you'd be here says."

"When mom called and told me the shock news well or else would I be.'

"Shocking news?"

"Yeah, shocking"

Letty this is Rebecca Whitmore, and Rebecca this is my pain in the ass baby sister."

Rebecca put out a hand and was envelope in a bear hug. Rebecca was a little shocked at first, but the warmth coming from Clancy sister. Was the real thing.

"We are going to be great friends. I thought it would take an act of Congress to get all clanker married off and you managed literally overnight."

"Clinker?"

"Yep, it's to sound his brain make when he tries to think."

"Okay," said Clancy," enough of that."

"Oh, I don't know I kinda like it." Giggled Rebecca.

"Great double teamed again." Said Clancy." Did you bring the kids?"

"Jack couldn't make it he's got way too much school. But the girls are here.

 They"re in the kitchen with grandma."

After the fiasco with Willie Johnson, Letty had gone to Western Illinois University where she majored in accounting and business. It was there she met Dan Cummings a graduate student in engineering. After graduating, They were married. Dad took a job with the firm in Chicago while Letty worke. for a suburban accounting firm. Dan took to Jack and Dan to Jack ,they had Jessica two years later followed by Beth Ann.. The girls were now seven and five. By all accounts, a handful. When they saw Clancy they both ran at him.

"Uncle Clancy." They both shouted as they jumped into his arms. Clancy picked each of them up in one arm and twirled them around. Both girls giggled and laughed and hugged Clancy by the neck.

"I've missed you two leprechauns."

"Were not leprechauns uncle Clancy." Said Beth

"well then how else do you account for being so short?"

"I'm only five Uncle Clancy. I'm big for my age

Clancy laughed, the girls laughed, everybody laughed.

Clancy Caudle look in Rebecca's eyes.

"What." He said.

"So, you're good with children to."

"Only these two, and Jack.'

"You can't forget Jack uncle Clancy." Said Jessi.

"These are big brother." Said Beth to Rebecca." He looks after us."

"I would never forget Jack. Jack's a hero, right?"

That's right the girls." Said both girls at once.

"Two years ago Jack was almost killed saving Bethann. She had run into the street Jack grabbed a just-in-time since then he's been there knight in shining armor he's really good to them to. Got more of his uncle in him than his father.

"Letty." Said Clancy," were going to have to talk about Willie before you go back to Chicago.'

"What's he done now?"

"Later"

'So you've only come to play with the kids?"

"Of course." Said Clancy.

Elizabeth Ryan ignored her son and gave Rebecca a big hug.

"Is amazing is this all seems, it kind of makes sense to me. It would take an extraordinary woman to make my son see the light."

'Thank you Mrs. Ryan, I'm a little amazed myself.'

"Beth, please?"

"Of course."

"Clancy, since you're the only man available would you open the wine bottles,

while Rebecca and I talk." Said Beth Ryan as she led Rebecca to the kitchen.

"I never thought Clancy would ever as someone to marry. I'm a firm believer in marriage. And I truly hope that this marriage will be a blessed one.

"Thank you."

"Do you have any idea when?"

"None whatsoever. Maybe June. That way everybody will know I'm not pregnant"

"Well thank God for that."

"Oh, I'm sorry, I didn't mean..."

"No, don't worry, dear. Water under the bridge. Dan's a good man, and he's taking Jack for his own, far enough away from that no account Johnson boy. Well you know."

There was a long moment of silence before Beth spoke again.

"What do your parents think about all this?"

Rebecca sighed," I haven't told them yet. I will as soon as I figure out what to say."

"Just tell them. I'm sure the love Clancy. He really is a good man."

"I know, but you don't know how Boston Irish Catholics can be."

"I'm Irish, and Catholic and I was born in Middleburg, Massachusetts."

"No kidding, my aunt Sissy lives in Middleburg."

"Small world is getting smaller.'

'Still, I'll have to be creative with my mother. But you're right, the love Clancy."

Just about then the timer went off.

"Dinner is served.' Said Beth.

"What can I do," ask Rebecca.

"Well, take this and this and let's go." She said as she handed Rebecca to side dishes.

In the dining room Clancy and Leddi were getting the girls settled, everything was ready. Little Beth reached for a dinner roll. The older Beth said, "we say grace in this house Elizabeth Ann. Little Beth pulled her hand back and set up right.' Sorry grandma."

Grace was said, the wine was poured, food was served, everybody dug in.

Clancy's mother and sister told every story about Clancy they could think of, embarrassing Clancy to no end, Rebecca felt so at home she leaned into Clancy and said," this is wonderful. I was so worried about coming here.

"It's the way we've always been. Life is for the living was my dad's mantra, he was never one to put on airs, always tried to give a guy a break."

"To miss him.'

"Every day."

After dinner Mrs. Ryan put the girls to cleaning the table. Rebecca insisted on helping, saying that her mother always threatened no dessert for anyone who didn't help.

"So what's the big secret?"

"Not here not in front of mom and the girls. Let's go out on the front porch."

"Jake Turner was found murdered Saturday afternoon."

"No you think will have something to do with that?"

"I don't know yet, but there is some evidence that points to him."

"What does he say?"

"That's just it, is run off. We traced them to Chicago as of yesterday. The worst part of the is he ran off with Turner's wif."

"Judge Penny Brooke gave old Horace 48 hours to bring him in. Old Horace took that time to get will out of town."

'If Will comes around you'll call the police. I'm having a hard time thinking Will would kill a man, but until I know for sure I have to go by the book."

"Well, he hasn't seen his son in five years. Why would he come by now?"

"I don't know, I don't think you will, but I thought you needed to know."

"Thanks Clancy, by the way I really like your doctor. She's great."

"I know, was really surprising how much mom has taken to her. Who would've thought?"

"Hope you get the same treatment from her parents."

"I got a in, her dad's a gator."

"Oh God." Left Letty," let's go back inside get some of that dessert."

Later as Clancy and Rebecca were leaving, Beth said to Rebecca," call your mom she should know what daughters been doing."

"I will. I was hoping Clancy to come to Boston with me. That way I'd have backup."

"Call her, then I can to."

"What for?" Said Clancy.

'" Curiosity mostly, mothers of the intended, so to speak.

Chapter 38

Once in the car, Rebecca was quiet.

"It's up hon?"

"How ever am I going to tell my mother that after two days in town I'm engaged to the local sheriff and involved in a murder case?"

"You that scared of her?"

"Not at all, but she's a formidable woman and somewhat old-fashioned. This just may knock her for a loop."

What if we take off Friday, drive to Chicago and hop on a plane to Boston. We could be there by dinner, sort of surprised them."

"You do that for me?"

"Sure, I've always wanted to see Boston. You said your dad goes to the Red Sox games."

"Red Sox, Celtics, Patriots, Bruins, Boston College, Harvard, you name it they go."

"Think about it. That will give me three days to solve this case."

"Yeah, less time than it takes to get engaged."

She had him in the arm as hard as she could.

"What is with you and all this hitting."

"I got three brothers, I learned how to be preemptive."

Chapter 39

Later that night as Clancy and Rebecca slept curled up together, the phone rang.

"Sheriff Ryan."

"Sheriff, this is Hank Brown. We just pulled Jimmy Turner out of a wreck out near his farm. We couldn't find Dr. Whitman. Dr. Hamilton is at the clinic. He's in pretty bad shape but still alive."

"I'm on my way."

"What is a Clancy?"

"They just pulled Jimmy Turner out of a wreck. He's at the clinic."

"I'm coming to."

What they showed up together it to in the morning, more than one deputy had a puzzled look on his face. None more so than Dr. Hamilton.

"We called Mrs. Wilson. "She said you hadn't been there all day."

"She was with me."

"Deputy Brown said he woke you up."

"He did."

"Okay, okay, please don't ask questions Dr. Hamilton." This might seem a little strange to you, I assure, you it's more than a little strange to us."

"I mean, Clancy and I have decided to get married."

Dumbfounded was a good word, stupefied was a little better, overwhelmed.

There you go.

"What do you mean, married/"

"Were getting a lot of that." Said Clancy." It's pretty simple to grasp, married is married."

"Your mother, Clancy."

"She knows, she's okay with it."

"I'm sorry Rebecca, but you just hit me right between the eyes."

"If I thought I could explain, I would. It's just one of those things."

"Okay," said the doc as he threw up his hands," let's go see our patient.'

Jimmy Turner was be to hell. Multiple cuts and bruises. Broken jaw, ribs left arm. X-rays had shown internal damages.

"We need to get him to a trauma center, now." Said Dr. Hamilton.

Clancy keyed his radio," County one to dispatch."

"Go ahead Sheriff.'

"I need an ambulance at the clinic right now"

There was a short pause, the deputy came back on the phone, and said," it's on Its Way, Sheriff."

When the evidence got there they loaded Turner in.

Dr. Hamilton said," one of us needs to go with him. One of us needs open the clinic."

"I'll go with Turner." Said Rebecca.

"I was hoping you'd say that." Said Clancy I'll follow you to the emergency room. Lights and sirens all the way. We're have to go to Peoria."

To Rebecca he said," if he comes to. Find out what you can. I'm not buying the car wreck. I'll have Hank ride with you. I'll be in the truck right behind you.

"Got it Sheriff."

The image took off Clancy turned to the remaining deputies and asked," tell me what you know."

"Deputy Walker said," I was the first one on the scene we were doing our regular drive by the Turner place. We found the wreck, it looked like he just drove into the woods. No skidmarks or anything."

"That's right Sheriff." Said Brown.

"Realized this one. Didn't appear drunk either."

"All right, make sure you put it on the report I want to see it first thing in the morning."

Chapter 40

The ambulance beat Clancy to the trauma center by about 10 minutes. Jimmy Turner was in the emergency room while Rebecca was busy signing him in..

"Hey." Said Clancy as he walked up next to Rebecca.

"Hi, almost done here." She said "Did he ever come to?"

"Yeah. For a minute or two."

"Say anything?"

"Nothing that made any sense., He said it was them you want my land. Then he drifted off. The last thing he said was they killed Jake. By then we were here."

"Wanted his land, who would want his land?"

"Developers maybe?"

"Mike was telling me that Mayor toms and old Horace were working on a deal to build a factory near the Turner place tomorrow I will talk to the mayor and old Horace."

Clancy turned to the receptionist and said"this is a criminal investigation. Nobody sees him. Can you keep his name quiet?"

"Sure. Dr. Whitmore signed them in as a John Doe."

"Really?" He said turning to Rebecca," good thinking."

"I thought if someone was trying to kill him, they might try again."

"Where's Hank Brown?"

"Downstairs with the EMT's. They decided to wait for you."

"I'll go find them and send them home." Said Clancy.

To the receptionist she said," Do you have any security that could watch the patient?"

"We have a secured wing where we put patients who need to be watched."

"Good, thank you

"I'll go talk to Hank and beat you back here."

"Okay, I want to talk to the doctor before we go."

Clancy went looking for Hank in the EMTs while Rebecca went looking for the doctors that treated Jimmy Turner.

"How is he Dr.?"

"Pretty banged up. He's going to make it though."

"Do you think his injuries are consistent with a car accident?"

"Maybe, but there are some injuries that might not be explained away by a car accident. There was some small pieces of wood in the head wound."

"Did you save them?"

"Yes." He said as he handed her a small bag with several splinters in it.

"I'd say the head wound was a result of blunt force trauma. Maybe a baseball bat or some other type of wood."

"Thank you Dr.. Would it be possible to get a report on all this as soon as I can?"

"Sure. I'll write it up and fax it over as soon as we're done here."

Chapter 41

It was almost daybreak when Clancy and Rebecca got back to McAbee. They decided to crash for a few hours and just go in late. People would just have to get over it.

Clancy finally dropped Rebecca at the clinic a little after 10 AM then went looking for the mayor.

He found the mayor in his office. He was shouting at somebody on the other end of the phone.

"Look, the answer is no and it will always be no. I can't and I won't. I don't have…"

He stopped talking as soon as he saw Clancy standing there.

"Good morning Sheriff." He said, "I'll call you back." He said to the phone.

"Sheriff, you can't go around manhandling your deputy. There are rules about things like that."

"If you're talking about your son, he's lucky he still has a job."

"Please, so he made a little joke."

"Bullshit." Clancy yelled," he scared Dr. Whitmore to death."

"I'm sure you just misinterpreted what he said."

"Okay, you can tell him for me I'm going to reassign him to the night shift in the jail. I'm also going to promote Hank Brown to chief deputy."

"You can't do that, I won't allow it."

"Once again, I don't work for you. I am the duly elected sheriff and I run the Sheriff's office. I'll do what I think is best."

"It sounds like you taking this way to personal."

"Well you're going to find out soon enough. Rebecca and I are engaged to be married and Junior made some very rude and dirty comments about her, so yeah it's personal."

Before the mayor could say a word, Clancy said," I want to know all about the factory deal you an old Horace have going."

"How do you know about that?'

"It's nothing, just exploratory. There's nothing for you to be concerned about."

"Bull shit. Here's what I know. I know you've already applied to the county for rezoning. I know that your got Mike Billings doing the legal work to get it done. I know that the property are looking at is that parcels south of town owned by old Horace. I know that it butts up against the Turner farm. I know that one of the Turner brothers has been murdered and the other wasn't in town 24 hours ago when somebody tried to beat him to death with a baseball bat."

"I heard it was a car accident," said the mayor, looking somewhat whiter than usual.

"You heard wrong. It was a setup to look like an accident. And lastly, I know what Jimmy Turner said before he left into a coma."

"What did he say?"

"That's my business. Now, you're going to help me with this. Or should I consider you a suspect"

"Suspect, I'm the mayor."

"So."

"Okay, okay, there is a deal. It's all but done, you're right. It will be great for McAbee, great for the whole county,, new jobs, new housing, new taxes. Everybody benefits."

"So why all the secrecy. I only found out about it yesterday."

"It's the way they wanted it."

"All nice and quiet, so the farms around the facility would never know, no chance to protest or anything."

"No no, nothing like that."

"Does in the county board have to hold open meetings in order to rezone farmland?"

"Of course. It's all planned for Thursday night."

"Really, seems no one but you knows this little minor fact. Where are the posted notices. Did you make sure all the area farms were told or were they just be in the way."

"Sheriff, you're accusing me of conspiring against my own people."

"Sure sounds that way to me."

Before the mayor could say another word Clancy got up and walked out leaving Toms grasping for breath.

Clancy stopped at the county clerk's office next.

"Marge," he said." I need to see the surveys for the south quarter of the County and the ownership plate to."

." I don't have them. Mike took them last Friday and hasn't brought them back yet."

Next stop, Mike Billings office.

"Mike, do you still have the surveys."

"Yeah, look at this"he said as he unrolled the maps.

"Here's old Horace's land, and here's the Turner place. Do you see it."

"No. See what?"

"Old Horace's property has limited access. Only a small area as any connection to the roads..Also look here."

He pointed to what was a rail line running along the opposite side of the Turner land.

"This rail spur is as far from Horace's land as it could get. But the Turner land would be perfect."

"Can we get a warrant to search the Turner farm?"

"I'll bet we can."

Mike dialed the judge's office spoke to the clerk who put them through. To the judge Mike explained the situation and got a warrant to search all of the Turner farm "Great." Said Clancy." Let's keep is very quiet till we go."

"I'll get the warrants you round up the troops." Said Mike.

Clancy next went to the police office.

"Can I have today's duty roster?"

There were 18 officers on duty including Tom Junior.

"Where's Junior?"

"In the call room doing nothing as usual."

"Calling for me, in my office."

"Clancy?"

"What?"

"Well, I don't want to get him in trouble."

"He's already in trouble."

"He's been talking about Dr. Whitmore."

"How so?"

"Saying she's been hitting on him. Told some of the guys he was, in his words mind you, going to get him some of that real soon."

"Thanks for telling me this. I want you to contact each person I checked on the duty roster. Get them into the call room. Within the hour Call Hank Brown at home and get him in here to."

"Okay, what's going on?"

He spotted JR heading towards him." In my office." he said.

Chapter 42

Clancy was sitting on his desk when Junior came in.

"You wanted to see me Sheriff?"

"Please sit on deputy Toms."

"Deputy Toms?"

Clancy handed Junior a piece of paper that had the county logo at the top.

"Notice of suspension." Clancy said.

"Whats this, you can't suspend me."

"I can and I have. You are hereby notified of the suspension of two days without pay. You are furthermore relieved of any and all duties as chief deputy. Your new assignment will start at 10 PM Thursday where you will take over as the night jail guard from Thursday through Monday 10 PM to 6 AM. Any questions?"

Junior was speechless." You can't do this to me. My oh man won't allow this."

"Like I told him I don't work for your father and I don't answer to them either."

"I refuse, I won't do it."

Clancy took a pad of paper and a pen out of his desk, he slid it across the desk to his ex-chief deputy.

"What's this for," he bellowed." I'm not going to resign."

"You just refused a direct order from your superior officer. Insubordination is a fireable offense, I'm giving you two options, comply or quit. Choose."

"Fine, I'll comply. But this isn't over."

Junior got up to leave. Clancy stopped him at the door.

"I'll need your gun, badge and radio on my desk, now."

Junior looked stricken what he laid each piece down and stood staring at the sheriff.

Clancy stood up closed the door and got up close and personal with Junior.

"I want you to know something. Dr. Whitmore has agreed to be my wife. So you won't be getting some any time ever. If I so much as here of any small impropriety about my future wife I'll forget about this badge and I'll rip you a new ass hole, you got it."

Junior didn't answer.

"I need an answer, boy"

"I got it."

Clancy open the door and called to one of his officers. "Ofc. Walker escort deputy Toms out of the building and follow him home."

"What?" Deputy Walker looked confused.

"Now."

"Yes sir."

Chapter 42

Half an hour later the men are all assembled in the call room. Hank Brown looked almost dead but made it in.

"Hank,could I see you in my office?"

"Sure."

After Clancy had closed the door he said." Remember what I said yesterday about the new opening?"

"Yeah, you said I should apply."

"I just demoted Tom Junior. I want you to take over as our chief deputy. You want the job."

"Me, right now?"

"Yes, we are about to exercise a search warrant on the Turner farm. I need you to take command. You can do this, I see it in you."

"Okay, but you gotta tell the men. It'll mean more coming from you."

"Not a problem." Clancy said as he pulled chief deputy badge from his desk.

"Put this on your shirt and come with me."

Clancy entered the call room followed by first deputy Brown. Every eye in the room saw the new badge Brown was wearing."

"As of today." Clancy began." I have relieved deputy Toms of all duties relating to chief deputy. In his stead I have promoted deputy Hank Brown to this post. I expect all members of the Maccabee County Sheriff's Department to show our new chief deputy the respect his new office deserves. Any one of you who is of a like mind with deputy Toms views, should at this time, begin looking for new work outside of law enforcement."

Mike Billings was sitting in the back of the room waving the warrant.

Clancy nodded at him and said "I've called you all here because I know each of you personally and I trust each of you I know you are dedicated to this county and to this department."

"Today we are going to exercise a search warrant on the Turner farm you 10+ chief deputy Brown and myself will conduct the search I've asked the state police for assistance they are sending a 12 man entrance team from the regional SWAT headquarters. They and not us will exercise the warrant. If there is any gunfire from the farm all and I mean all Maccabee County deputies will fall back and secure the perimeter is this clear?"

"Yes sir." Said Hank Brown." Let's look at the map."

Clancy laid out what he thought would contain the people at the farm. 20 minutes later the call came telling them that the state troopers were ready and in place.

"All right everybody, it's Showtime." Called Clancy.

As each man left the room Clancy checked the vests all were wearing them.

Smart guys". Clancy thought.

The met up with the SWAT team just outside of town They had been waiting at the maintenance building to avoid notice. The trip to the Turner's farm was only a few minutes away so there was a little time to think about the job ahead Clancy hope secrecy

had been maintained last thing he wanted was a welcoming committee soon you know soon enough.

Clancy hoped secrecy had been maintained Last thing he wanted was a welcoming committee. He'd know soon enough.

As they approached the farm each of the deputies went to their assigned place. Effectively blocking any and all escape routes the SWAT team slammed down the drive into the farm we came to a halt in front of the main house. The emptied the truck and spread out.

Four troopers in full riot gear approach the front door..

"Open up, State police we have a warrant to search these premises."

No answer. theycalled out again. Still, no answer.

The SWAT commander gave the okay to break down the door. Using a battering ram, the door was crushed in. All of the SWAT men poured inside shouting andspreading out through the house.

The house was empty as were the trailers and the barns.

The SWAT commander called down to Clancy. "Sheriff, this place is abandoned.

No people, no bikes, nothing.

10-4 captain, were coming up."

The place was indeed empty. No people, no bikes, nothing.

"Okay, I want this place searched from top to bottom. Be careful, no telling what they left behind."

Clancy Stood with the SWAT captian and Hank Brown as the men moved out.

"Think they were tipped off?" Clancy asked Hank.

"Hard to say,Sheriff I thought we had this contained.

"Send a couple of guys over to Rollie's. See if there are any of his boys out there.

And send someone back into town just to look around. These people didn't just disappear."

"Right Sheriff."

"Sheriff," called one of his men." You might want to see this."

He was calling from one of the trailers. The insides were full of what can only be what one would call a drug lab. The whole thing have been left behind in a hurry "Had to be tiped." Said the SWAT captain.

"It would seem so. Can you get a crew down here to take this all apart"

"Yeah, we got a special crew for that. I'll get it: going."

There were so many different types of pots pans and drums to go over. Clancy was looking at whatseemed like microwave oven when he saw it.

"Everybody out now," screamed Clancy. "Out, get out get out now."

Clancy was screaming and waving his hands." Everybody get back to the cars."

Everybody Clancy could see was running back towards the road when it blew. The fireball was enormous. The force of the explosion a Clancy off his feet. The SWAT captain. Landed a few feet away.

Clancy felt as if the air had been sucked out of his lungs. He lay still for a moment to he was able to get his bearing, then he jumped up.

"Headcount," he yelled the SWAT And was up and running towards his been.

After all the men had been accounted for, Clancy went to each man to check for injuries. Mostly minor cuts and a few scrapes.

"We were damn lucky." Said the captain." What did you see?"

"I don't really know," said Clancy." A brick of clay and a timing device counting down to zero. Must have been C4 or something like that."

"We're going to have to call the ATF on this one. If it was C4 it can be traced back to its manufacturer."

Hank Brown came over to Clancy and said," that was set off to go while we were here. They had to know we were coming."

Clancy pulled Hank away from the others." I want you to talk to each man. See who they talk to. When we get back to the station, talk to everyone there. Somebody knows something."

"Got it Sheriff." Said Brown the captain was busy talking on his cell phone. When he finished, he turned to Clancy and said"ATF has been notified. They want us to pull back to the road and secure the area. They're sending in a bomb squad."

"Hank, pull a man back. As you talk to them send them out here who secure the area. These people went somewhere. You stay here, keep Stone with you. Call me later when our if you know anything new."

Clancy turned to the captain," I'm leaving my chief and another deputy here.

Whatever you need talk to Hank. And he'll get it done "Sheriff," said the captain. "You save some lives out there today mine included. I just wanted to say thanks."

He shook Clancy's hand and walked away.

Chapter 43

Clancy got back to his office and went looking for Mike.

"He's not here, he went to see the judge right after you called."

"Will you tell them I need to see him as soon as he gets back."

 Back in his office, Clancy closed the door, leaned back in his chair and closed his eyes and thought "This case was getting out of hand." He was at the point where you can't tell if you're asleep or not, when the phone rang.

"Sheriff Ryan"

"Sheriff, it's Michael's here. I'm over at Rollie's. The bikers were all here last night saying goodbyes to all the staff "Did they say where there were going, or why?"

"Yeah. They all thought that Turner was selling out. Rollie thinks they're going back to the Twin Cities."

"Good work, write it up and give it to me as soon as you can."

Chapter 44

Mike Billings was currently seated Judge Pennybrook's chambers and the judge was not happy.

"You're going to have to explain this to me, Counselor." He began." A booby-trapped drug lab not 10 miles outside of town."

"It was in a tractor-trailer. Very easy to move around. It's in pieces now."

"And you think the biker gang blew up the lab before they left?"

"That's one theory. I for one don't think the leave it all behind. It was mobile,

They could have taken it anywhere they wanted."

"So what happened?"

"I think they got scared off by something."

"Like?"

"Like, whoever killed Jake Turner and nearly beat his brother to death."

"And just who might that be?"

"Were working on it. It might have something to do with the new factory deal."

"How so?" Asked the judge.

"The proximity of the land to the highway and the fact that the Turner place would be a better site for the factory. We need to look at who's going to build this place."

"It's a company from New Jersey. They make doors and windows. Doesn't seem like they'd be involved in a murder."

"Can we get a background check on these people?"

"Yes, I think we should know just to were dealing with. I'll call the states attorneys office. In Springfield see what they have on this company. You do the same with the New Jersey office."

"I've got to see Clancy," said Mike." He should be back from the Turners by now."

"Call me when you know something."

Chapter 45

Microphone Clancy in the call room trying to get the pop machine to work.

" Damn machinery, all I want is a soda."

Mike walked up and hit the machine just below the coin slot. In A&W root beer popped out.

"Amazing. How'd you do that?"

"It's all in the wrists," laughed Mike.

"How's Pennybrook?"

"Pissed. Doesn't think were doing enough."

"He's right. I just don't know what to do."

"Were going to look into the factory people, see what shakes."

"Good idea. I should hear from ATF pretty soon, till then I'm going home."

Before he left he called the hospital in Peoria to see how Jimmy Turner was. He was told that there was no change. Then he called the clinic, but Rebecca was with a patient. He told Jean to tell Rebecca he was going home and she could call him there.

Chapter 46

It was almost 330 before he finally got home. He let gator out and just sat on the deck. Bone tired from the day and unable to think about what he should do next.

He must've nodded off, because the next thing he felt was warm and wet.

"Gator get off of me." He said as he was coming out of his sleep."

"So that's what you really think of me?" Laughed Rebecca.

"Oh God. I'm sorry, I just thought... I guess I was asleep."

"I guess," she smirked." I stopped and picked up some steaks. You know how to use a big grill out there?"

"I sure do, we could eat out here."

"That would be nice."

As they went about preparing dinner, Clancy couldn't stop thinking how truly wonderful Rebecca was. Out of the corner of her eyes she caught him watching her.

"What?"

Clancy caught off guard said," nothing I ah..."

"Come on, out with it, what?"

"I was just thinking that if this is how I'm going to spend the rest of my life, I'll be the luckiest man on the planet."

Rebecca slowly walked towards him kissed him on the neck in a way that made his knees buckle.

"You keep talking like that, your luck is going to start tonight."

Clancy smiled, and hugged her tight, still somewhat overwhelmed by it all. He knew he was.

Later that fall after all was put away, Clancy and Rebecca were sitting quietly, down wreck room when Gator began to growl.

"What is it boy?"

The dog was up on all 4 feet now. Clancy said to Rebecca," stay here." As he headed up the stairs. Listen to minutes later Rebecca followed. Clancy was standing in the living room with the lights off looking through the drapes.

"What is it?" She asked.

"Someone's out in the yard, and thanks for staying downstairs."

Sorry, but you you've already died on me once this week."

The first shot shattered the front window glass. Clancy threw Rebecca to the floor and rolled her, away from the window putting his body between Rebecca and the window just about were Clancy's head the second shot hit the window frame about were Clancy had just been.

Clancy grabbed his gun off the table where he had left it and crawled to the window just in time to see the shadow of a pickup squealing out of sight.

"What was that all about?" Asked Rebecca looking a bit pale.

"I think we were just warned." Replied Clancy.

"About What?"

Clancy had bent downed to look at the damage done by the shooting.

"This whole case is getting odder and odder."

Clancy picked up the phone and called the dispatch. Two minutes later for Sheriff cars pulled up in front of his house."

"What the hell happened?"asked Hank Brown.

Apparently, this must have been a warning, maybe trying to scare us off the case said Clancy's anger showing to his usual calm "What you want us to do Sheriff?"

"Get the tax out here. Get the bullets. Call Jeff Simons at the hardware store to fix the window, just boarded up today. Afterwards will get the glass fixed.

"Got it."

"Next, I want to know the whereabouts of Tom Junior."

"You don't think..."

"I don't know, but he's really is that me pissed at me."

And Hank Brown began to make his phone calls, Clancy turned to Rebecca.

"Maybe you should go to Mrs. Wilson's boardinghouse?"

"Sure, I can go later in the dark, wide awake and worry about you. Sounds good."

Clancy was not in a laughing mood, but that made him smile.

"I guess I'm just going to get used to not being the boss of my own home anymore."

"What's that supposed to mean." Said Rebecca, looking a bit put out.

"There is a reason I never found any of the local women of any interest. Most of the women around here were raised to be housewives and mothers, not partners. I don't want to subservient wife, I want an equal."

"That's very refreshing coming from a man in your position."

"It's the truth. When I was in college I dated a lot. Mostly cheerleaders and sorority girls, but I always found myself attracted to the women who were trying to get something more than just a husband."

"So you're saying you like strong women not showpieces."

"Look at Bea, smartest girl in school coming from ISU ,up a degree in sociology from ISU. Gave up everything to be a housewife."

"Maybe, it's what she wanted."

"That's possible, but I would have bet the farm on a professional career when we graduated from high school."

"Things change, I was a cheerleader in high school."

"Really, high school is different than college.Cheerleading in college is a professional job."

"I know."

"Still you're right. I do tend to go for brains over beauty."

"What about Bea? She told me she had a crush on you since the fourth grade."

"I know, but she was Letty's best friend. It was a line you didn't cross."

"Why?"

"The best friend law.' "Never date sisters of best friends."

"I'm still not getting it."

"It's simple. You don't date your best friend sister. If two people are best friends guys mostly, but it could apply the women. If your best friend has a sister that you're hot for, he can't date her. Someone's always good to feel left out it's a no-win scenario tell me any of your brothers ever date one of your best friends?'

"No."

"Any of your brothers friends ever ask you out?"

"No."

"Best friend law, it's harder for guys who have friends with hot sisters."

"Why?"

"Guys who sleep with their best friend sister, better be prepared for a serious ass kicking."

"What about you and Will Johnson?"

Clancy grunted a small smile."and said, " Beat them right into his tuxedo."

They were both laughing at that when the phone began to ring.

"Sheriff Ryan."

"Hey Clancy it's me."

"Willie ,Where the hell are you?"

"I'm back in town. I'm going to turn myself in, but Clancy, I didn't kill Jake."

"I think we know about that but there's a connection we need to talk about. You come in first thing, okay. We'll stay low because something isn't right about this."

"Okay, but I really don't know much about anything."

"We'll see. Stay home, keep your head down and come in early."

Chapter 47

The guys from the board up service refinishing the Windows and Hank Brown had finances calls.

"You want me to station a car outside here tonight?"

"No, what I want is for you to tell each car working town tonight to cruise by here every 20 minutes or so. Get every license plate number of any car in the neighborhood."

"Got it."

"And send someone out to the Johnson's farm. Make sure they're all safe out there."

"Got it."

"Did you ever find Junior?"

"Yeah, been out at Rollie's all night."

"Are you sure?"

"Got it straight from Webster. he saw him out there."

"Okay, good nigh,t chief deputy."

"Good night Sheriff and good night Dr. Whitmore."

"Good night Hank."

After Hank had left Clancy turned to Rebecca and said, "I'm beginning to think I made the right decision about Hank."

Chapter 48

Clancy had hardly been asleep for long when he was awoken by the sound of the phone ringing. Rebecca, lying beside him was breathing slow and deep beside. As she ,slept beside himsimply marveled at how beautiful she really was.

The phone would not stop ringing.

"Ryan, what?"

"Sheriff, this is Webster. We got shots fired at the Johnson farm. I called dispatch and that I called you."

"Okay, wait for backup. Don't go in by yourself. I'll call dispatch and see you out there."

"Okay." He said and then hang up."

Rebecca was stirring now. Clancy stood up as she rose to one elbow.

"Shots fired at the Johnson farm. I'm going out there," Rebecca began to get up," I'm going to, they may need medical help."

"I was hoping you'd say that."

Clancy called the office and got through to the night dispatch, dispatch told him that three cards at only been sent out.

"Tell them not to approach the farm until there all together."

"10-4 Sheriff."

"Ready." He said to Rebecca.

"I'm ready, do we have the stopping get my medical kit. It's in my van"

"Sure it's kind on the way."

"Let's go."

They got Rebecca's kit made it to the farm in 20 minutes. By the time they got there the whole place was lit up."

"What happened?" Clancy asked the deputy left at the gate.

"I'm not really sure Sheriff.I think someone was shot."

"Where?"

"Up by the big barn eggs up there now, the large one. Hanks up there now."

"Good, stay here. Don't let anyone in or out."

The drove up the main drive to where the police cars were gathered. Chief Deputy Brown saw the Sheriff and waved him over to where he was.

"Over here, Sheriff."

"When we got here?"

"From what we we've been able to piece together, Thom Billings and Will Johnson were inside Thom's place." He said as he pointed to the apartment over the garages." Thom said he heard the horses spoke, decided to take a look. When they got to the barn they saw two guys inside. Thom said they look like bikers."

"How did they know they were bikers?"

"Thom said they had on the usual gear, jeans, boots, leather jackets."

"Do they recognize them?"

"No, said he didn't think they were from the Turner bunch."

"Where's Thom now?"

"In the main house. Got a small flesh wound in the upper arm."

"And Willie?"

"Don't know and no one is saying,"

"Great," said Clancy." Just marvelous."

"I'm going to go and take a look at Thom's arm." Said Rebecca.

"Good. See if you can get them to tell you what happened to Willie?"

"So you want me to sweettalk him?" She said as she walked away.

Clancy did answer.

"What happened next." Apparently, Willie yelled at them to stop. One of them turned and fired a shot hitting Thom. So far that's all I've got ."

"Okay, it would be daylight soon. I want to complete canvas. Footprints, and car tracks. get as good a description as Thom can give you."

"Thom said they had what looked like gas cans."

"Really, think they were going to torch the place?"

"That's with Thom thought."

"If they had guns, why didn't they just shoot them?"

"I think Willie return fire."

"What, how do you know this?"

"Look here Sheriff." Said Hank as he pointed to several places that looked like bulletholes.

"If the bikers were here and Tom and Willie were over by the door, than these holes were made by either Tom or Willie."

"Right, what does Thom say?"

"Nothing, says he wants to talk to his nephew."

"Did anyone call Mike?"

"Yeah he's on his way"

"Let's go talk to Thom."

Inside they found Thom Billings being attended to by Rebecca old Horace and Jack Johnson were standing back letting her do her work. Old Horace looked like he wanted to bite somebody.

"So Sheriff, what's this county come into where were not safe in our own homes?"He said.

"This whole deal stinks Horace, I'm gonna find out what's going on here and who's to blame."

"You'd better."

"Is that so?" Clancy said ,As he took steps towards Horace." Maybe you'd like to explain why you got Willie out of town after you promised the judge to bring him on Monday? I believe today is Wednesday."

"I don't know where Willie is."

"Bullshit."

"You can't talk to me like that Sheriff."

"Deputy Brown, arrest Horace on suspicion of harboring a fugitive and for obstruction of a police officer in the performance of his duty."

"You can't do that."

"I can and I will. Where's Willie."

Old Horace didn't answer right away. This may Clancy even madder.

"Where's Willie?" He barked.

"I don't know."

"Take them in deputy. I'm sure the judge will see him by Friday" Deputy Brown move forward and said, "Please place your hands behind your back."

"Sheriff, I protest." Said old Horace.

"Where's Willie?"

"He's at the south line shack." Said Jack Johnson." I said in there myself."

"Jack?" said old Horace.

"Sorry Dad, I'm not going to let them take you to jail."

"Sheriff?" Said Deputy Brown, looking at the sheriff."

"Let them go for now   ," Said Clancy. "Take Webster and picked up Will. Bring him here."

After deputy Brown left, Clancy turned to Thom.

"So are you gonna tell me what happened here?"

"I'm waiting for my nephew."

"Mike can act on your behalf, he's the counties attorney."

"Still, I'd like him to be here."

"Will you answer some simple questions?"

"I suppose."

"Did you recognize any of the guys in the barn?"

"No."

"Would you know them if they were part of the Turner gang?"

"Yeah, They weren't."

"Are you sure?"

"Yeah, I'm sure. I've been drinking with those guys all summer. These guys were not from the farm."

Clancy turned to Willie's father and grandfather and said. "We think Willie was set up to take the fall for Jake Turner's murder. We think it has something to do with the new factory deal. What can you tell me about that?"

"Pearson Windows has been shopping around for around piece of land within McAbee and five of the border counties. About six months ago Mayor toms came to me with this deal. Thought that I might be able to help work it out. Seems he really wants to have that factory in MacAbee County. We show the people from Pearson around and the piece that would fit their needs was my land south of town. What it would have seal the deal was the Esther place. Mayor Toms, myself and a lawyer from the Pearson company went to make an offer to buy the place., Esther, who was nearly 80 years old, agreed.

A week later she was dead and the Turner boys were moving in. Told us they had different ideas.

"Yeah, we found the meth lab out there yesterday. It was rigged to blowup. We barely got out of there in time."

Thom Billings had a look of astonishment on his face.

"You got some you want to say, Thom?' Said Clancy.

"Meth lab. Those guys were way too stupid to do any sort of chemistry. They were just mules. That's all they were, mules."

"You seem awfully familiar with all this." Said Clancy." Can you prove any of this?"

"No, but I know they got their drugs from St. Louis and then took them up to the Twin Cities or Chicago. That's all I know."

"And how do you explain the lab we found?" Asked Clancy.

"What kind of lab?"

"It was in a kind of mobile home on wheels."

"No, the only mobile home out there was the one the guys lived in. They took it with them."

"Do you know why they left so Suddenly?"

"Yeah I do. Bulldog, one of the bikers, told me he thought Jake was kille because he shorted a haul." Then, when Jimmy went missing, they panicked and ran."

"County two to County one." Came the squawk from Clancy's radio.

"County one here." Replied Clancy.

"We've located Mr. Johnson but is unwilling to come along peacefully."

"Aw man," said Clancy. Then into his mic he said, "stay there, I'm coming to you."

"County one to 17, Webster you copy?"

"Yes Sheriff, go ahead."

"When you talk to Rollie the other day, did he think the bikers were running."

"Yes Sir Sheriff, he said they were scared to death."

"Thanks, out."

Clancy thought for a moment and then said, "all of you wait here. I'm going to go get Willie and them were all going to sit here and figure this thing out."

As Clancy was pulling out, Mike Billings.

Pulled in alongside what's going on here Clancy?"

"I can't tell you just yet, but I'm getting closer. I got to go up and talk Willie out of the old line shack. Thom's inside. Go talk to him. There's something he's not elling us."

"Okay. Come back quick. I got news to."

Out at the shed, deputies Brown and Webster, were standing beside their cars.

I He still in there," asked Clancy.

"Yeah said he'll shoot anyone who comes close."

"Jezz, never was that smart, was he?"

"I guess not." Replied Brown.

Clancy just walked up to the door and began to beat on it.

"Open up Willie. Its Clancy,? You going to shoot me?"

After a minute, Clancy said, "Now Willi, I don't have all fucking day."

"Okay, okay, I'm coming."

Clancy stood back as the door slowly opened.

"Gun first Will."

A 9 mm hit the dirt as Willie came out with his hands up.

"Put those down you dumb fuck. I should kick your sorry ass for all the bullshit you put me through."

"I'm really sorry Clancy, this all just got out a hand somehow."

"Come on back to the house we've got to figure this all out."

Once in the squad car, Willie turned a Clancy and said," I totally screwed this up Clancy. That bitch, Mary Beth Turner, disappeared as soon as I got her to Chicago."

"What about the blood at the holiday express?"

"Mary Beth and I had sex twice there. I got up to pee, and while I was in the bathroom, she started to scream. I ran back, he was covered with blood and screaming at the top of her lungs. I wanted to take her to Dr. Hamilton's, which she said Jake would find them there. She wanted to go to Chicago, said it would br safer there. Soon as we got to Chicago she said she was feeling better. Said she just needed to rest. After she laid down, I went out to buy some aspirin and some beer. That's when I called you.

When I got back, she was gone. Took everything, My money and my car. Had to wire Old Horace for bus fare. Thom pick me up in Peoria.

"There's one thing we've got to clear up. How did your pearl handled bowie knife end up stalking Jake Turner?"

"How should I know? It got taken away from you last Friday."

"By who?"

"Your chief deputy, that's who."

"Ex-chief deputy. Are you telling me that Junior took it in as property?"

"No, I'm telling you he took it. When I asked for it back, he said it was police property now."

Willie looked over at Clancy and didn't like what he saw.

"Clancy, look like you're going to explode."

Clancy was close to boiling over, but he got it. He knew what was going on now

"Clancy, do you think Mary Beth set me up?"

"Yes I do."

"Then where did all that blood come from?"

"Rebecca said it was consistent with menstrual blood but look older. She sent a sample to be tested. We should know soon."

"Rebecca?"

"Rebecca Whitmore, the new Dr. that Dr. Hamilton brought in to take over for him."

"And where at Rebecca already?"

"I'll tell you the whole story as soon as we get this mess cleared up. She's at your house right now fixing up your uncle Thom."

"Thom got hit?"

"Yeah, but he's okay. Tell me did you shoot back?"

"Hell yeah, hit one to."

"What, you telling me you think you hit one?"

"I knew I had him, spun him like a top."

"Shit Willie, why didn't you say so right at the start." Clancy said as he grabbed for his microphone. "County one to dispatch."

"Go ahead, Sheriff."

"Get on the phones, call every medical facility in the county. Were looking for a possible gunshot wound or anyone buying medical supplies in quantity. This is an armed and dangerous felony, So tell everyone to be on their toes."

"Got it Sheriff."

"So, is she cute?"

"Gorgeous."

"Really?"

"Think she'd like an old farm boy like me?"

"No."

"What do you mean no? Come on Clancy, what aren't you telling me?"

"Well, okay, were a sort of engaged to be married."

After several long minutes of drop jaw staring, Willie said."Mar-Mar, married, married?"

"Yes."

"She's only been in town, what, five days?"

"Well truthfully, I asked her last Sunday night."

"I'm feeling a little faint here. You're telling me that it only took one day for great Clancy Ryan to get engaged to a woman he'd never met before. In one day?"

"Yeah, so?"

"Be a hell of a woman?"

"She's more than even that."

"So now I'm going to have to rethink my whole entire life."

"You need to get a life first.'

"Funny guy. You're full of it today aren't you?"

When Clancy and Willie got back to the farmhouse, Clancy gathered everybody together.

"Okay," said Clancy, "let's see if we can pull this thing together. Here's what I know. We got one dead Turner brothers and one brother in a coma. I've a gang of bikers who ran off scared to death of something. I got Jake's wife involved in setting up Willie and now she's run off. I got a real estate deal that went south because the owner of the property died and the Turner gang moved in. I've got a murder weapon that was supposed to be in police custody, but was found 4 miles outside of town stuck in Jake Turner's ribs. And to top that off I got a meth lab that almost blew me to hell that, Johnson says shouldn't of been there."

"What do you mean, shouldn't of been there?' Asked Mike.

"There was no lab, I was there on Friday. No lab, no trailer." said Thom.

"Mike, you said you had news?" Asked Clancy.

"Yea, Rebecca was right. It was menstrual blood. It was just like you **thought** It was four-day old cows blood."

"Hank, put out a warrant for the arrest of Mary Beth Turner, charge of conspiracy to commit murder. Call the Minnesota State police. Let them know we think the gang is Is headed their way."

"Got it.'

"Rebecca, was there a bulletin Thom's arm?'

"Yes, I have it here." She said as she held up a baggie with a bulletin it.

"Compare this one to the ones we dug out of my house."

Rebecca handed Hank the baggie with the bullet in it, when she saw Willie staring at her.

"What?"

"You got any sisters?"

"Nope, three brothers." She laughed as she turned a Clancy. "I guess you told him."

"Yeah, between Mike, Willie and me, we've been friends since before we were born.

"And I will live to be 1 million years old before I'll ever get over this." Said Willie.

"What's to get over?" Asked Rebecca." Do you really think we choose who we all in love with?"

"Hell, I follow love all the time," Said Willie." But it wears off sooner or later."

"Excuse me," said Clancy. "Try not talking to Willie Rebecca. You'll be much better off."

"Yeah, he likes to bring people down to his level. Right around the third grade."

Said Mike with a smile.

"Funny guys." He said looking at Rebecca," they were always jealous of me.'

"Oh Yeah, I could definitely see that." Said Rebecca with a roll of her eyes.

Willie just shook his head. He knew right there he was overmatched.

"Horace, tell me how this deal came to you."

"Mayor Toms said he was contacted by a lawyer from Pearson looking for property to build a new factory here. Wanted to know what I thought about selling some land."

"And you said you had a deal with Esther, right?"

"Right."

" Her dying and leaving the farm to the Turner's, ruined the deal.

"Yep."

"Mayor say anything?"

"He was mad as hell. I think he really wanted this."

"Enough to murder someone?"

"That, I couldn't tell you."

"What about Junior? He said something to me this morning. He said 'you'll see soon enough.' See what?"

"Maybe I can help you with that," Said Mike.

"What do you got?"

"Two weeks ago, Junior came by my office, asking a lot of legal questions."

"Like what?"

"You wanted to know about seizure of private property by the government. I told him about eminent domain and how it worked. I told him it was a slow process and has to go through the courts. Then he asked me about the RICO laws."

"What's RICO?" Asked Willie.

"It's a law enacted during the 80s that allows the government to seize private property if it is proven the property was used in the commission of a felony. It was used mostly against organized crime."

"Bingo," Said Clancy.

Mike nodded, then said," it's a lot clearer now.. The bigger cities use it all time.

Get caught drug dealing drugs from your car, they take your car. Run a meth lab from your house, they take your house."

"And the law applies to farmland as well I assume."said Clancy.

"So you're thinking the Turner's were set up?" Asked old Horace.

"Yes I do," said Clancy.

"But that only makes sense if the two properties were sold together." Said old Horace.

"What you mean?"

When we thought the deal was going to fall apart, we signed the land over to Willie. He's got a deal going with the Bristol co-op. They want to lease the land for a test site for hybrid corn production."

"Who knew this, Mike?"

"No, I was working under the assumption the deal was still going forward."

"Without the Esther farm the deal was dead. We knew this months ago." Said old Horace "Let me get this straight," said Clancy as he turned to Old Horace." You knew the deal was dead without the Esther's land and Mike was under the assumption that things were still going forward, right?"

"Yeah, and the deal with the co-op. Was a done deal next week, were signing the papers," Said Willie.

"This doesn't add up," said Clancy." Why would the County attorney be working on a deal that everyone, but him, knew to be dead?"

He was looking straight at Mike Billings.

"Look, as far as I knew the deal was still going."

"And what made you think that?"

"Mayor Toms, he was under the impression that the Johnson land was all that was necessary."

"But he knew that the Parsons people wanted both pieces."

"And if the co-op deal went through, then the whole mess falls apart."

"Willie," asked Rebecca." How long was Mary Beth married to Jake?"

"I don't know that they were."

"Bikers don't marry, it's all common law. Get on the back of a man's bike you took his name for as long as it lasted."

"So how long were they together?"

"I really don't know."

"I do, said Thom Billings." She came back with them from the big bike rally in South Dakota."

"When was that?" asked Clancy.

"First part of August."

"Shit," said Clancy." It was a setup from the start. When did you first start up with Mary Beth." Willie?"

Willie was busy looking down at her shoes.

"Willie, when?"

"First part of August, almost as soon as she got here." Willie said sheepishly.

"So, is here to help set up the Turner's, when it's found out that Willie is going to lease his land to the co-op. The fight at Rollie's makes it look like you and Turner had it out over Mary Beth. She then fakes, what seems to be a miscarriage and gets you to drive her to Chicago." Turned to Rebecca and asked," how my doing so far?"

"I'd say you were right on except for one thing."

"What's that??"

"Where did she come from, who sent her and who's she working for?"

"Yeah, and I'm thinking those two goons came with her. We should get fingerprint information back today, find out who she really is."

Willie was still looking down at shoes. It was finally sinking in just what happened to him.

"I don't get it," he said." If the deal was dead, why go to all this trouble?"

"Maybe the deal wasn't dead," said old Horace. "What if someone told the Pearson people that they could still get the land for them?"

"Who?"

"My first guess would be Thomas Thomas Senior."

"That's nuts." Said Mike." For what reason?"

"What time is it?" asked Clancy.

"Almost 7 o'clock," said Rebecca.

"Does Thom need any more medical attention?"

"No, but I would like to see him at the office sometime tomorrow."

"Hank, gather up all the evidence and get a call into the FBI. Then let's see about these fingerprints."

He started to say something else, but before he could get a word in a call came from over the radio.

"Dispatch to County one."

"County one here."

"Sheriff, we just got a call about a break-in at the pharmacy over in Bristol.

We've got cars on the scene. They think they've got one inside still."

"Hank, forget about the evidence. Give it all to Webster. Get over to Bristol and take charge. I want you to get these mutts."

"Got it."

"Alive. The careful. These guys are shooters."

"I got it."

Hank bolted out the door, jumped in his car was gone. Webster started to gather up the evidence. Clancy paused for a moment, took a deep breath and said.

"Willie, stay here for now. Don't go anywhere. Mike and I are going to see our mayor."

"Clancy." Said Rebecca. " If this break-in is our guy, and one of them was shot."

"Right, we need him alive. Let's go. Mike do me a favor. When you get to your office, call Pearson. See if any promises were made and by whom. Wait till I get back go see the mayor together."

"Sure Clancy, I'm a little pissed off here. If Toms put my office in the middle of all this I'm personally going to kick his ass."

"Right." Said Clancy and Willie at the same time.

Chapter 49

By the time they got to Bristol, Hank had the entire place cordoned off. The By more than a dozen pharmacy was surrounded.Police car's.

"What if we got here Hank?" Said Clancy.

"At least one guy inside, maybe both, but we've only seen one."

"Okay, let's go get this guy."

"Don't you want to wait for the state SWAT team?"

"Let's see if we can talk to them first."

Clancy walked to the side of the building yelled in." You, in the store, this is Sheriff Ryan. Can you hear me?"

"I hear you." Came a raspy, shaky voice.

"I have a doctor with me, you sound pretty banged up."

"Sure, send him in."

"Now you know I'm not going to do that. You're going to have to come out."

"I can't, I'm shot."

"Well, you're going to bleed to death in there. Where's your partner?"

"Gone, left me."

"Now that sucks. Just can't trust anyone these days. Look, the way I see it you got two choices. You can go to jail or you're going to die."

It was dead quiet for several minutes. After what seemed like an eternity the the door opened and a handgun was thrown out into the sidewalk

"Okay, hold your fire, I'm coming out."

"Okay everybody, backup and hold your fire."

Slowly everybody backed up as the door opened. The biker, clearly wounded, walked out, leaning a on a crutch taken from the store.

"Hold it right there." Yelled Clancy as he pointed his gun at the suspect. "Stop right there."

Clancy and Hank were cautiously moving forward when the first shot rang out.

It came over Clancy shoulder and hit the biker square in the chest, blowing him back into the store. Clancy and Hank while everybody else outside hit the ground.

Clancy's first thought was 'where was Rebecca.' He couldn't see her. When he turned his attention to the following biker, his first thought was, didn't look good.

"Who hired you?" He screamed. "Who?"

"Mary Beth Turner." Came a very weak response.

"Who hired her?"

"Don't know, don't care." And he was out.

Clancy reached down the feel for a pulse, found none as Rebecca came running through the open door.

"Are you nuts? There is an active shooter out there."

"Nice to see you too." Came the retort. "The way you went through the door I didn't know who was shot, besides you have a wounded man in here."

"I think he's dead."

Rebecca knelt down felt his p pulse and said. "Not yet."

"County one to County EMTs. Get in here."

Two minutes later EMTs came in with their kits and a stretcher. Rebecca began and went to work on the biker.

"Did anyone see the shooter?" Asked Clancy.

"No, but we got the gun, shooter left it behind." Said the deputy.

No one saw the shooter and the gun was left behind. Clancy began to scan the crowd, wondering if the shooter was still out there.

"Transport him to to Peoria general, cover his head on the way out."

"What are you thinking Sheriff?" Asked Hank.

"The shooter could still be out there and we just may know him."

Now Hank was scanning the crowd as he slid closer to the door frame.

"Rebecca, do you have a solution for gunpowder residue?"

"Yeah, but if it was a bold action hunting rifle, there won't be as much as there would be if it were a pistol."

"We'll do it anyway. Hank, line up all the deputies and anyone out there we might know."

"Got it."

The biker was transported include critical condition, while Clancy sprayed each person with the chemical, but no tested positive.

"Could of worn gloves." Said Hank.

"Yeah, gloves," Clancy said as he scanned the crowd again. He wasn't liking what he was thinking.

"Okay." He finally said. "Let's get this cleaned up and get back to town."

Rebecca, who at first wanted to go with the shooting victim, decided to go back to town with Clancy. It was nearly noon before they finally got to their respective offices.

"Haven't we been here before?"asked Rebecca as she got out at the clinic.

"Great, I think you owe me a dinner out tonight."

"Sounds great. We need to talk about something important tonight."

"What?"

"Tonight."

"I can't do that. That's all I'll be thinking about all day. It will affect my work."

"It's nothing earth shattering. It's just that I'm worried that after this all settles down you may find our town a little boring."

"Our town or you?"

"I'm just a country boy at heart."

"Hey, I don't have all the answers, but I'll tell you one thing. Never in all my days would I have thought I'd agree to marry a man I just met. But here I am. It's not the town or the case, it's just you. Call it Providence or fate whatever you like. Things change over time. So in about 40 to 45 years I may feel different. So why don't we just wait till then okay."

"Okay, do you think you could handle moving in?"

"Yep, sooner or later I will, but let's give it a little more time. I haven't been to Mrs. Wilson's since Saturday night.

"That's what I mean."

"And I don't see that changing, but if I keep my room at the B&B for now.

I'll feel better okay?"

"Okay, what about we try Millie's again?"

"Sure, I should be done by 530."

Chapter 50

When Clancy got to the station he headed towards Mike's office. Mike was there on the phone.

"This is a criminal investigation. Your help would be much appreciated I understand that but I need to know I think will all pass that now. Okay I'll be calling back."

Mike slammed down the phone." Assholes are stonewalling us."

"What they say?"

"Nothing, after talking to four different people I got nothing they said they get his company involved in a murder back to me their in-house counsel said he knew of no existing and didn't want his company involved in a murder."

"Can we pressure them?"

"I don't know, it's not like were some big city task force."

"I might have an idea on that.Were close enough to Chicago or St. Louis, to get some press if we handle it right. you know, 'Murder a Small Town.'

Might just get people interested, then you tell Parsons will keep their name out of it for a little cooperation."

"Might work, but first I'd like to talk to Mayor Thomas."

"Me too. But first I need to talk to deputy Brown."

Chapter 51

Clancy stuck his head into the dispatch office and said," you see Hank?"

"Try the jail office."

"Thanks."

Clancy found Hank going over the evidence collected during the last few days.

"What you got Hank?"

"Well the bullets match, so we only got one shooter."

"I thought so."

Hank pulled a file folder office desk and handed it to Clancy.

"This our interest you."

"What is it?"

"We got a hit on the fingerprints left at the motel room."

"Really?"Said Clancy, as he began to read.

"Mary Elizabeth Morelli, age 28, born in Trenton New Jersey. Now that's interesting."

"Yeah, look who her father is?"

"Victor Marelli. Sounds familiar."

"Jersey crime boss some say he's a guy Tony Sparano was modeled after."

"Hold on here, what the hell is the daughter of a New Jersey Mafia boss doing in McAbee?"

"And you should also know that the Pearson's headquarters is also in Trenton New Jersey."

Clancy picked up the phone and dialed Mike," Mary Beth Turner is really Mary Elizabeth Morelli daughter of Victor Marelli, a crime boss out of, now get this, out of Trenton, New Jersey."

"You've got to be kidding me. Now or in the Mafia?"

"So it seems."

"Okay that fits Chicago cops found Willie's car in the long term parking lot at O'Hare airport. She could be anywhere by now."

"Forget about her, we've got a bigger problem, like what's the Mafia doing in McAbee?"

"Time to call in the feds."

"Remember Dan Blackmore?"

"Yes. Special Agent out of Chicago, nice guy."

"I'll call the Trenton police."

Chapter 52

Clancy went back to his office where he updated his case file with what he had learned. He had told dispatch to get him through to the Trenton police. The call came10 minutes later.

"Hello. This is Sheriff Clancy rhyme from the Maccabee County Illinois to whom am I my speaking with?"

"Hello Sheriff Ryan, this is Capt. Barron, Trenton police. How may I be of service to you?"

Clancy laid out everything he knew about Marinelli and the case, including the pearson window involvement.

After Clancy was done, Capt. Barron said, "Two things, Victor Marinelli is a lowlife thug. He got his start back in the 60s. You name it he's done it. We've been after him for years. Secondly Pearson Windows is a mob front, it's true they make Windows and doors, but it's owned by the mob."

"What would they be doing out here?"

"I don't know but it can't be legit. Nothing this bunch does is on the up and up."

"I know it's a longshot, but I have an arrest warrant for a Mary Beth Marinelli.

Could you look into her whereabouts for me?"

"Gladly, I'll fax you the file on Pearsons to."

"Great, thanks, you been a huge help Capt."

Chapter 53

Mike Billings was having better luck talking to Dan Blackmore. It had been several years since they spoke, But Blackmore had remembered him.

"Well you're right about one thing, we be very interested in this case." He said after Mike had told him the case history.

"Let me talk to my boss but we're in, trust me. I'll call you back as soon as I have something."

"Pearson Windows is a mob front." Said Clancy.

"I think were getting in little deep here."

"I know, what did agent Blackmore say?"

"He thinks they'll come in. He's taking it up the ladder, but doesn't see a problem."

"Good, let's go rattle the mayor."

Chapter 54

Mayor Tom's was on the phone when Clancy and Mike walked in. He immediately hung up the phone without say another word.

"Sheriff Ryan I need to talk to you." He said showing signs of anger.

"Whatever." Clancy said as he held up his hand to stop Tom's.

"First we've got to get this out of the way."

He reached into his pocket and pulled out a handheld tape recorder push the record button and said,

"First interview. Please state your name, age, occupation, and home address."

"What the hell is this. I will not." He said as he stood up.

Clancy who was almost a foot taller, stood also.

"Do it." Clancy demanded.

"You can't talk to me like this," he said looking at Michael.

"I do what he says mayor he's been shot at twice almost blown up and had his house shot to hell. Probably not a good idea to piss him off"

"Name?"

"Thomas A Thomas."

"Age?"

"54."

"Occupation?"

"Mayor of the town of McAbee Illinois."

"Address?'

"147 N. Lansing, McAbee Illinois."

"Mr. Thomas you have the right to remain silent. Anything you say can and will be used against you in the court of law. You have the right to an attorney. If you cannot afford one, one will be provided to you. Do you understand these rights?"

"What's this all about?"

"Do you understand these rights?"

"Yes."

"Yes what?"

"Yes, I understand my rights."

"Good," said Clancy. "Tell me all you know about Victor Marinelli."

Mayor Tom Thomas White, sat down hard and said nothing.

"Are you refusing to answer the question?"

"I don't know anyone by that name."

"Sure you do Tommy boy. His daughter was in our jail last Friday night. It took me a little while to find this out. Seems the fingerprint card which is required for all arrests has gone missing. Michael, who was unveiled duty that night?"

"I believe it was Tom Thomas Jr. are mayor's own son."

"Why that's right. You haven't seen your son recently have you? We seem to be having a hard time find him."

"I, ah, I don't know where he is. You demoted him. Who gave you the right?"

"The voters of Maccabee County. The same one to throw you on your fat ass once I tell them how you tried to help the New Jersey Mafia come into our County."

Mayor Tom's was like he was going to faint.

"I, I, I," he stammered.

"Okay Tommy, let's spell it out. Victor Marinelli is the head of the Trenton New Jersey Mafia family that owns the Pearson door and window company. His daughter Mary Elizabeth Marinelli, is also known as Mary Beth Turner. Let me ask you questions to Thomas, how does a girl from New Jersey hook up with a guy at the Black Hills bike rally who just happens to be the half owner and a piece of property her father company has just failed to acquire?"

"I'm sure I have no idea."

"Let's continue. This same woman comes to town with bleach blond hair and a new last name and immediately takes up with the owner of the second piece of land her father failed to acquire. Do you believe in coincidence Mr. Thomas?"

"Could happen, I suppose."

"You suppose? Not me, it was a setup from the start. And who was it that brought Pearson door and window into Maccabee County? Well, Tommy boy?"

"They came to me."

"Did they?" Clancy asked.

"Tell me, Mike, what would be the first thing that you do if a company that size keep knocking on your door?"

"Run a background check."

"And do that here McAbee?"

"That would be me."

"And did you?"

"No."

"Why not?"

"I was assured that it was all being done."

"Assured, by whom?"

"Mayor Tom Thomas."

"So mayor, you got anything you'd like to add to this?' Added Clancy.

"Tom," said Mike." This may be your only chance stay out of. We've already call the FBI. We will be hearing from them today, and they don't cut any deals.

"I, I don't know what to say."

"Start at the beginning." Said Clancy.

"Are you sure that Marinelli is Mafia?"

"Absolutely."

"Can you turn the recorder off?"

"I don't think so. Let's hear what you have to say,then we'll talk."

What the mayor had to say wasn't much, he was playing stupid card for them.

"I didn't know no one told me." He said giving them nothing new.

They came to him, he didn't know Marinelli, didn't know anything about Marinelli's daughter. After he finished he said," that's all I know. I swear."

"Okay then, I guess we'll just go to the media. Going to be a great story," said Clancy.

"Wait a minute, just wait," Tom cried. "You can't do that. This is a small town, people will think I did this."

"Then tell us the truth," said Mike.

"I told you the truth."

"Let's go Mike," Clancy said." Will tell the FBI Tommy boy is stonewalling us.

That should make things real interesting."

"What to do Ryan, you want to be mayor to?"

"No I don't. I'm just trying to find out who's fucking up my County, and you're refusing to help me. Makes you look real guilty doesn't?"

With that Clancy started to walk out. As he got to the door he turned and said, "I want JD in my office today or he's done got it?"

"You can't fire him." said the mayor.

"Fire him, I'm going to arrested." With that, Clancy turned and left.

"Is he serious?" Said the mayor.

"As a car wreck,"said Mike. "You had your chance to tell them what you know.

He just wants the truth.

"Mike you gotta believe me. Marinelli was only a name to me. I have no idea how this got so screwed up."

"I'd like to believe you Tom, but someone inside is pulling the strings and were going to find out who it is."

Chapter 55

Those who knew Clancy well knew him to be an easy-going likable guy. They also knew not to piss him off. Once he got on the other side of his Irish temper there was no calming and down. But a time Clancy got back to his office he was seriously pissed off. Someone in the county government was helping the Mafia. One person was dead and now he had two people in the hospital.

Clancy was pacing back and forth across the front of his desk phone rang.

"Sheriff Ryan." He said rather loudly.

"Hmm, maybe I should call back later?" Said Rebecca. "What's the matter?"

"Is nothing sweetheart. The current event is getting to me I suppose?"

"Did you just call me, Sweetheart?" He said with a slight laugh.

"Yeah I guess I did it, is it a problem?" The sound of her voice was beginning to have a calming effect.

"Not at all, seems kind of natural like you ment it."

"hmmm."

"Hmmm,thats all you got to say?"

"Got lost in thought,sorry."

"Care to share?"

"You always been called Rebecca?"

"Well yeah, I'm not much of a Becky."

"No,"

"My dad called me Bacca when I was young and the only other name is Reba.

That's a no for the obviously reasons."

"There can only be one Reba."

"You are such a hick."

"Hey, name callingalready."

Clancy's anger had melted away talking to this wonderful woman.

"So did you call me for a reason or just to bust my balls?"

"I just got a call from Peoria general, Jimmy Turner is awake."

"How's dinner in Peoria sound to you?"

"I can get away by 430."

"I'll see you then."

Chapter 56

By 4 o'clock Clancy was getting hot again. He'd make sure Mayor toms got the message about Junior, but Junior hadn't shown yet.He picked up his phone and called Mike.

"Anywhere in Junior yet?"

"Nothing, it's like he fell off the end of the earth."

"If he was working with the mob guys they might want to cut the loose ends."

"Jezz, you don't think?"

"I don't know. Where the hell is he? One other thing, Jimmy Turner is awake.

Don't tell anyone,there still a shooter out there. I don't want him trying to finish off Jimmy or his partner."

"Partner?"

"Yeah the guy we pulled out of the pharmacy still alive thanks to Rebecca."

"Where is he?"

"Locked away. If he survives I'm going to get to him."

"Get to him, what's that supposed to me?"

"I need answers, he's got him. I need them and then going to get them."

Chapter 57

Clancy was just hanging up the phone when someone knocked on his door. He was surprised to see Tom Junior.

"My dad said you're going to arrest me. That true Clancy?"

"No. You're an ass hole but your a loyal asshole.. Someone on the inside of this department is helping the crooks and I need your help."

"You demoted me."

"Yep and that's while my plan will work."

Chapter 58

2000 miles away in Trenton New Jersey, the phone on Vincent Marinelli's desk rang.

"Yeah."

"Mr. Marinelli. Boy is still alive."

"How do you know this?"

"It's a small town in a small Sheriff's Department. I have my sources."

"I don't like loose ends. Take care of this today."

"What can I do? He's under police guard."

"You put them there in the first place. If you had handled this right in the first place we wouldn't have this problem."

"It was a clean shot. How was I supposed to know the new doctor would be with the sheriff?"

"This is not my problem. It's yours. Take care of it or you'll become a loose end."

Chapter 59

Clancy picked up Rebecca at exactly 430. The drive to the hospital should've taken 75 minutes he made it in 50. Jimmy Turner was still hooked up to all the machinery but was sitting up eating Jell-O.

"Good evening Sheriff, you come all this way to see me?"

"Odd as it may seem, yeah we did."

"Who's the pretty lady?"

"This is Dr. Whitmore. You can thank her for saving your sorry ass."

"Well then thank you Dr. maybe I could thank you a little personally, if I ever get out of here."

The cold silence in the room. Jimmy Turner looked up at the Sheriff, he did not like the look Sheriff eyes

"Or maybe not."

"Who beat you up Jimmy?"

"Don't really know. I was sitting around drinking with the two new guys next thing I know I was in here. They tell me that was two days ago."

"Tell me about the new guys?"

"Didn't really know them, came in with Mary Beth, Jake's new wife. They didn't seem like bikers, acted more like mob muscle.

Jimmy was quiet for a while then he said," they tried to kill me didn't?"

"Yeah,we think so."

"Why?"

"Were not sure yet,complicated. We think this they killed Jake to."

"Motherfuckers," Jake said quietly under his breath.

"You be happy to know one of them is downstairs all shot up."

"You do this?"

"No, but I'm going to find out real soon."

Almost on cue Capt. Angelo of the state security team, with two heavily armed members of his squad.

"Evening Sheriff."

Chapter 60

Downstairs near the end emergency room entrance unseen by the security team a man dressed in black slipped into the hospital, found the stairs and went up. No one is at and waited the third floor nurses station. He was able to find the room he was looking.

So he slipped back into the staorwell and waited.

Chapter 61

"Going on Clancy," asked Rebecca. The site of the armed men frightened her.

"Going to catch us a mole Everything ready Capt.?"

"Yep, he won't get away."

"Okay let's go." He turned to Rebecca and and said," I really need you to stay here. These two gentlemen are here to protect you.Please stay with her them.okay?"

"What's going on Clancy?" She Said, a little more forcefully this time.

"We think an attempt will be made to try and kill our shooter. We plan to stop it."

Chapter 62

In the small stairwell, the man in black waited. Sooner or later one of the guards would have to get up, when he did, the man can make his move. So we waited.

Just as he predicted, the security guard got up and went down the hall. He pulled his ski mask down over his face slowly pushed open the stairwell door. Slowly made his way down the hall looking left and right you walk past the room. Believing that the area was safe he went to the room. At the door, he looked around one more time, and pulled the mask down over his face so that only his eyes showed.

The room was pitch black. Only the outline of the target could be seen. As he approached the body on the bed, he pulled out a 6 inch stiletto his jacket, open the blade and moved closer to the man in bed. He was about to finish what he had come for when all the lights in the room suddenly came on.

"You probably want to rethink that deputy." Said Clancy."

The man, who still had his back to the door, considered his options. Seeing that he had none, he dropped the knife and turned around coming face-to-face with the Maccabee County Sheriff and the captain of the state SWAT group, as well as two heavily armed men pointing machine guns at him.

Clancy step forward and went to pull the mask off the man.

"Let's see who we got here." He said, as he pulled the stocking cap off.

God, I hate it when I'm right." He said as he looked into the face of deputy Arnie Webster, who had been in on all almost every phase of this case.

Clancy hit Webster as hard as he knew how rate in the nose. A crisp breaking sound could be heard almost all the way down the hall as the blood began to flow.

"Deputy Thomas take this piece is shit into custody."

"With pleasure Sheriff," said Tom Junior.

Chapter 63

Clancy and Rebecca had found a small restaurant not far from the hospital Clancy had ordered a huge stake was not very interested in eating it.

"Man I trusted Webster I would not have believe that if I hadn't seen it in my with my own eyes. Hell I just hired him."

Clancy stops on.

"What?   Said Rebecca.

"I just hired him." Said Clancy with a look of utter amazement on his face.

"When?"

Jesus just before the Turner showed up. God dammit." Said Clancy.

"You think he was sent by the New Jersey people?"

"Seems likely, and I'm gonna find out."

"How did you know it was Webster?"

Process of elimination. It wasn't Junior or Hank. Those two guys have been with us for years, local boys I couldn't see either one of those is a killer. Webster was the only one else on duty Saturday morning. He's the only one that could have taken the files on Mary Beth Marinelli."

"How did you set this up so fast?"

"I didn't, I let Junior do it. That way I could go about my day like I didn't have a clue."

"Are you going to give him back his job."

Sure, Hank likes the night shift, Junior likes today's. I'll make them shift responsible chief deputy's."

"Good idea, when are you going to talk to Webster?"

"As soon as the FBI gets here. Agent Blackmore wants a crack at this guy. He's hoping he can get them to turn on Marinelli."

"Why don't you eat your steak and forget about all this for a while?"

Chapter 64

The next morning Clancy felt better bolstered by a good night sleep, he got to the office ready to kick some ass. He knew he had he knew who the killer was, who sent them. But he didn't know why. He just couldn't believe the theory that the whole thing was about a factory deal gone bad.

"Damn back more and his team should be here Sometime today." Thinking out loud. Maybe they can solve this for me."

On his way to his office he stopped by the mayor's office. Mayor toms did not look happy to see him.

"Well I hope you have come here to apologize?" Said the mayor.

"Why? you not to clear yet."

"You know I had nothing to do with this mess. I was just looking out for my town. Maybe a little overzealous, but never criminal."

"Relax, if I thought you were involved, I'd have never used Tom Junior to set this thing up. He'd have run to you so fast, shit. You'll be happy to know that I'm reinstating him as chief deputy for the dayshift, Hank Brown stay on as chief deputy for the night shift."

"Good, you're really scared him you know," "Maybe we'll start acting like a cop now? You tell them he needs to make nice nice with Dr. Whitmore."

"He knows that. That was pretty bad, wasn't it?"

"Yes it was. Look Tom, there's still one more rat in the kitchen and I'm gonna find him. Keep this under wraps."

Chapter 65

Damn Blackmore and his team arrived at noon. They tried to check in at Wilson's B&B but there wasn't enough room. Mrs. Wilson made a quick call to the clinic to ask Rebecca if she was still going to be using her room. Rebecca said yes but you can find different accommodations until the room was available again.

She went to the B&B to get what stuff she stills that had their by way of the Sheriff's office. Clancy had a big smile on his face.

"Was this year doing?" she snapped.as she slugged him in the arm.

"No, but I can't say I'm unhappy about it," he said after she told him what happened at the B&B.

"So you think I'm gonna stay at your house?"

"Not thinking, hoping," Clancy said as sincerely as he knew how.

"Yeah, well fine. There goes was left of my reputation."

Blackmore and his crew came out the front door. When he saw Dr. Whitmore he said," I am truly sorry Dr. I told Mrs. Wilson that we could double up and will probably only be here a few days.

"It's okay agent Blackmore, it was eventual that I be leaving the B&B anyway," she said giving Clancy a sideways look.

"Nevertheless Dr.we appreciate it."

Turning to Clancy he said," we got a hit on your guy in the hospital. Names John Raymond Stanley. Got a long rap sheet. Mostly strong armed stuff and two counts of possession of stolen goods."

"Anything on our fake deputy?"

"Nothing, it's like he doesn't exist."

"Our guide Mr. Raymond is still out of it, so let's start with Webster. Go to the jail and see chief deputy Thomas. He'll get it set up for you. I'll come by in an hour or so, so you can take your time and work your magic."

"My guess is this guy isn't going to cave to easily."

"Yeah, he's already asking for a lawyer. Until I know who he is I'm going to take my time asking the judge to appoint one."

"Better make it today."

"Yeah I know. Let me take care of a few things and then I'll go talk to the judge."

"About an hour also, okay Sheriff?"

Chapter 66

When Clancy and Rebecca got to Clancy's house she was still a little angry, the believing he got kicked out B&B.

"Really, as much as I'm happy about this, I didn't set you up. It's not my nature to lie to you."

"Maybe I'll stay in your guestroom."

"Fine." He said kind of surly "Oh no, you don't get to get mad at me. I'm going to get bounced around here."

Clancy put the truck into reverse and backed out of the driveway.

"Where are we going?"

When Clancy didn't answer he said even louder.

"Where are we going?"

"To my mother's, she has four bedrooms and I'm sure she'd love to have you."

Rebecca burst out laughing, so hard Clancy stopped the truck.

"What the hell so funny?"

"This is the new side of you are getting to see."

"What new side?"

"The wounded puppy."

"Great, now I am puppy."

Clancy was clearly upset, he set absolutely still, gripping the wheel, finally he said, "is it so bad a thing to want to come home each and every night to the woman I love. I don't have a lot of experience in this department. The last woma I lived with with my mother.."

"I've never lived with a man other than family. It's new to me to I guess I'm just a little scared."

"I'm sorry. If you not okay with this find you someplace else. I guess I got a little ahead of myself."

"No," said Rebecca Sternly, "I'm fine with it. We'll just have to work it out."

"Sure," he said."I told Dr. Hamilton I'd be back at 230. That gives about two hours to kill." She said with a look that made Clancy's heart pound.

Clancy pulled back into the driveway so fast Rebecca thought he was going to run right through the garage.

Chapter 67

Clancy got back to the office about half an hour later. He was an obvious good mood, or so we thought. His mood changed quickly when he met agent Blackmore just outside his office.

"Webster's dead. Shot in his cell." Said the agent.

"How the hell could that happen? Where's my chief deputy?"

"On his way to the hospital. Someone busted his head open."

"God dammit, how the hell could this happen?" Said Clancy mad as hell now, his good mood long forgotten.

"We had them down in interrogation, but he wouldn't talk. Said he wanted a lawyer. So we had your chief deputy take him back down to his cell. I sent agent Rodriguez to check on him after about 20 minutes. That's when we found the deputy unconscious on the floor and Webster dead."

Clancy grabbed the phone nearest to him and called the clinic. He told Rebecca the corner on this one what had happened and to come over said she had better bring Dr. Hamilton also.

"Were going to need the coroner on this one."

After Clancy hung up the phone agent Blackmore pulled him aside.

"Can we go someplace private?"

"My office."

After Clancy has shut the door, Agent Blackmore said," Clancy, you got a worm in your office. There's no way someone from the outside walking here and pulled the trigger and Webster. Had to be somebody on the inside. Somebody nobody thought out of place."

"This I already knew." Said Clancy." I was hoping Webster would give them up."

"Not gonna happen now."

There was a knock at the door

"Come in."

"Dr. Webb Whitmore and Dr. Hamilton are here," said the dispatcher.

"Good, I'll get them started. Be right back. Can you wait here for a minute Dan?"

"Be right here. Can I use your phone?"

"Sure."

Clancy led Rebecca and Dr. Hamilton down the stairs to the lock up. They found Blood Webster sitting on the bed, propped up against the wall. The front of his jail overalls were covered in blood. There was also at the desk, assuming deputy Thomase's.

"I'm going to let you work the scene here while I talk with Agent Blackmore.

When you're done here come by my office."

Rebecca who was already working the scene said, "could you put a guard on the door. Keep everyone out."

"Right," Clancy said as he turned to the deputy standing behind him." Stand your guard at the door, Nobody in or out, got it."

"Got it Sheriff, Sheriff, does anyone know how Tom is?"

"Not yet, I'll send word down as soon as I know."

"Think Sheriff."

On his way back to the office Clancy stopped at the dispatch.

"Call Hank Brown. Tell him I need him to come in. Tell them what happened if you need to be kidding here."

Back in his office Agent Blackmore had been going over the case file.

"Not much here Sheriff," he said.

"No. Maybe if we started Sat the beginning and go over piece by piece. You write down everything you know, and I'll write down everything I know. Once we have a good list will start comparing notes."

"Sounds like a plan."

Chapter 68

About 20 minutes after they got Starte, Hank Brown knocked on the door.

"When I was just a patrol officer I actually got time off."

"When this is over I'll be out by you and your wife dinner but until then you're on the clock. Think of all the overtime your booking."

"Great. My wife love all the extra money after I'm dead."

"Sit down take up a pad and pencil. Write down everything you can think of that may be important to this case."

For the next three hours they brainstormed, argued, wrote, argued somemore. In the end it came down to two things. They didn't know who was behind all this and what was so important to kill people over. No one believed it was all over a bad land deal.

Had to be more to it than that.

About an hour in Rebecca stop that Clancy's office to tell him they were done and that they were transporting the body to Thorson's for the autopsy.

As she closed the door, she said to Clancy," I'll see you at home okay?" And she was gone. Both agent Blackmore and chief deputy Brown looked at Clancy.

"What?"

"Home?" they both said in unison.

"Don't get your undies in a bunch were engaged."

"No shit?" Said Hank.

"No shit, now back to work."

By 6 o'clock that evening they were all so tired that they couldn't think anymore. Clancy called the dispatcher, who was getting ready to go home. He asked her to make a list of everyone known to be in the building at the time of the shooting. She came up with 23 names, including the FBI group.

"Scratch off all the women." Said Clancy.

"Why?" Said Dan.

"Not strong enough the cold clock Junior, plus most long-term employees over 40 years of age.

"Okay that's eight off."

"Four our deputies who were together at the time of the shooting."

"Okay, that makes 10 left."

"Three FBI guys."

"That's seven."

"The mayor's out, after all it was his kid that got clock."

"These three are County counselors were upstairs at the time."

"Three left."

"Jack is our chief janitor. 25 years on the job and his assistant is 64 years old, on the job for 20 years. Both retired deputies.

"That leaves only one name."

All three of the men stared at the last name. Clancy and Hank both looked at each other before Clancy said, "I won't believe this, I can't."

"I can't believe it either." said Hank.

"Well, said Blackmore, " This, doesn't make any kind of sense, does it?"

"But it does," said Hank. If you think in terms of access and foreknowledge."

"Hank," said Clancy, think about motive, Can you see one?"

"No, but that doesn't mean there isn't one."

"Dan," said Clancy. "I may have to turn this whole case over to the FBI and walk away."

"I understand that. I'm having a hard time this myself. I have no idea how to proceed. Do either of you?"

Neither of the other man had a clue. What would happen next was so outside of any of their collective experiences.

"Think motive," said Clancy.

"What motive," said Hank.

"Any motive. Write down anything you can think of."

"Power, money, maybe blackmail?"

"Maybe, but I just don't see it."

On it went until they had exhausted all possible motives.

"It's got to come back to the connection between Marinelli and the Turner's.

Maybe the land deal was a front for something else?" Said Dan.

"Like what?"

"I don't know, but if we could get a look at all the paperwork, maybe something will pop?"

"Hank, get the keys for the county clerk's office. Round up all the paperwork you can find on the proposed factory deal."

"Got it Sheriff."

Hank came back in about a half an hour with two full boxes of files, maps and folders.

"We may have to order out?" Said Dan.

"Yeah," said Clancy. But let's take everything over to my house. That way we could eat and work and quiet."

Clancy called the house but only got his machine. He then called the clinic, but Dr. Hamilton said that Rebecca left an hour ago.

"Something's not right." Said Clancy. "Rebecca should've gotten to my house an hour ago."

Hank picked up his portable radio off Clancy's desk and said, "County to do all cars in town. Be on the lookout for Dr. Whitmore or her van. Reported in when cited "10-4, 2." Came the call. "The van is still part in the clinic's parking lot."

"Shit."

Clancy began calling any place he thought she might have gone. He called his mother he called the B&B even called the grocery store. Finally he called back to the clinic.

"Hello Clancy," said the doctor. "I was just leaving."

"Rebecca is missing. We don't seem to be able to find her." Said Clancy.

"That's odd. Did you try Mike Billings?"

"Why?"

"He called just before she left. Said he has something to show her."

"Mike Billings called her?" He repeated as three sets of eyes turned down to the last name on the listed. Mike Billings.

Chapter 69

Rebecca knew her hands were tied and that she was blindfolded, but she didn't know where she was. What a strange sensation she thought. She knew she should be scared, but just wasn't. She knew she'd been adducted but not by whom or why. The last thing she remembered was putting the last of her boxes in the the van. She could still smell the ether on the cloth that someone put over her face, but that was all. Now she was lying on a bed or maybe just a mattress. She could hear someone talking or maybe two people but couldn't make out the words.

As she lay there the voices got louder. Two people arguing.

"Dumb fucking idea." Said the first voice. One she didn't know.

"What was, the kidnapping or the murders?" A man's voice, familiar but she couldn't place it.

Suddenly a loud bang, a gunshot she thought. Then no more voices.

Chapter 70

Clancy made it to the clinic in minutes. Rebecca's Van sat there in her spot. Inside were the boxes that Dr. Hamilton said she was moving. But where was she?

"Thus the car, make sure you do the back hatch," He told Hank.

Agent Blackmore had stay behind it station. He was calling in the troops under the likelihood that Rebecca Whitmore had been kidnapped. The first call the FBI station in Chicago. Requested and was granted additional man in a helicopter. Then with the help of the dispatcher he called every deputy not on duty, told him what was happening, and asked for their help. The first one to arrive was Tom Junior. In the back of his pickup were for the best looking hunting dogs in the county.

"Thought these boys could help." Was all he said. He had a huge bandage on his head.

"You going to be okay?" Asked Dan.

"Just a scratch. I want to help."

More people begin to show up at the station. The FBI helicopter was still an hour away. Agent Blackmore with help from Junior started to assign areas to the deputy's.

Several of the townspeople came in wanting to help. Seems the word had gotten out.

Agent Blackmore assigned to civilians and two deputies each of the areas.

"Stay two known areas to start with." He told them. "We looking for Dr. Rebecca Whitmore. She's 5 foot 10, about 135 pounds, auburn reddish hair worn mid-shoulder."

Agent Blackmore kept the name of the possible abductor self. Only Junior knew the truth and he had 12 stitches in the back of his head as proof.

Chapter 71

Back at the clinic Clancy and Hank were about to leave. The text were working the van and Clancy needed to get back to the jail. Just as they were getting ready to leave Dr. Hamilton came out of the clinic and flagged them down.

"Clancy you should see this." He said.

What he had was the preliminary report on the blood spatter found at the jail.

"Sent the samples by carrier. Haven't got the DNA profiles yet, but look at this."

What Clancy saw in the profile reports were three distinct blood types.

"Webster's juniors and the shooter."

"That's what I figured."

"good, how soon will we get the full profile?"

"Tomorrow afternoon would be my guess."

"So Junior must've got a shot off. Call the hospital, he said to Hank. See if he can talk."

"Don't bother Sheriff," said Dr. Hamilton. "Already tried. Junior checked himself out three hours ago ."

Clancy was about to tell Hank to call in but Hank was a step ahead of.

"County 2 to agent Blackmore."

"Go ahead 2."

"Seem to got a third missing person now."

"Who."

"Chief deputy Thomas. Seems he checked himself out of the hospital."

"No sir, he's right here helping to coordinate the search."

"Let me talk to him," said Clancy.

"This is County three."

"What the hell do you think you're doing deputy?" Clancy growled.

"Helping Sheriff, I need to make it right with the doctor. Can't do that if she's gone missing."

"Okay, you don't go running around. That's in order."

"Got it."

"One more thing. Did you get a shot in on the guys who hit you?"

"Sure did. Busted him right in the mouth just before we hit me with the pistol."

"So you're confirming who we think it was?"

"Yeah. It's deftly who we think it was."

Several of the deputies overheard the conversation they were looking for They stared at Junior looking for answers to who. Junior just shook his head and said.

"Not yet."

Chapter 72

Rebecca heard the footsteps coming towards her. She was sure guy wanted killed guide to. She was what she next? Whoever it was that grabbed her by the shoulder and and set her up to a sitting position. He could feel her his hands working on the blindfold knot, but when it fell off all she could see was the outline of her captor.

"What a fine mess you've caused Dr.." Came in all too familiar voice.

"Mike, What's going on? Why you doing this."

"You ruined everything."

"How? I didn't do anything."

"If you hadn't come to town this whole thing would have been so simple. Easy money."

"What money? What's this all about?"

"Maybe I'll tell you but first I've got things to do."

He pulled the can of ether out of his pocket and poured some into the cloth.

"No. No. You have to do that."

"Yes I do."

He grabbed her by the hair and smothered her face with the cloth.

Chapter 73

Clancy and Hank made it back to the station house just as Willy Johnson and Thom Billings showed up.

"Herd you might need some help." Said Willie.

"I told you to lay low. This is an over by a longshot."

"Me and Thom thought you could use all the help you could get."

Clancy took Willy by the arm and pulled him more than 25 feet away from the crowd.

"Willie we got a real big problem here."

"No shit."

"No, it's worse than that. Were about 95% sure it was Mike Billings behind this whole mess."

"The hell do you mean, Mike Billings?" He almost was shouting at this point.

"Quite down, I don't want anybody to know yet. I'm hanging in the 5%.."

Willie looked over at the crowd," What about Thom?"

"In close to you. I have no idea what to think yet."

Chapter 74

Mike Billings was driving south on Route 4 with Rebecca unconscious in the backseat. He knew where he was going, getting there was the trick. He assumed rightly, that the whole county would be looking for the pretty young Dr. it would be a bad idea to be stopped before he was ready, he was driving the speed limit acting as if nothing was wrong. He didn't think they were onto them yet but you can't be too sure.

Chapter 75

"Chopper in about five minutes." Said Agent Rodriguez."

Get two men on the ground and the chopper back in the air. Sheriff, who do you got who knows this County well enough to go airborne?"

"That would be me, Agent Blackmore," said Deputy Stone." I was with the hundred and first in Iraq spend a lot of time in chapters looking for people. I hunted these woods all my life."

"Sheriff?"

"Go."

The phone began to ring and Clancy grabbed a before it had a chance to ring a second time.

Clancy Dr. Hamilton here. Be Billings was just brought in. She's been beaten to a pulp and she's. Barely conscious, she said her husband did."

"Christ, there goes the 5%."

"Would set me?"

"Nothing, look Doc I'm going to send you a deputy.He'llstay with you until this is over. Maybe he can get a statement from Bea?

"Thank Sheriff, at this point I'll take all the help I can get."

" Wilkins, get over to the clinic, keeping an eye on Doc. Bea Billings was just brought in. She's been beaten up pretty bad. I'll need a statement if she's able."

He turned her Deputy Stone said," You heard that?"

"Yeah Bea Billings."

"Now you know who were looking for."

"You're kidding, right?"

"Not in the least. Find He's driving a red Ford expedition. Find him."

"Junior. Call them and tell him what's what."

"I'm on it Sheriff."

"Hank, go kick down the county attornies office door and find me anything that might explain what the hell is going on here."

"I have a key Sheriff."

"You have your orders."

"10-4 Sheriff."

"County 14 to County one." Came over the radio." Were out here at the Turner farm, we got a body. Looks like he's only been dead a short while."

"You know him?"

"Never seen them before."

"Might be the other shooter," said Agent Blackmore.

"Secure the area 14. No one in or out. Stay there until you're relieved."

"10-4 Sheriff. 14 out."

Chapter 76

When all the deputies left on their assignments, Clancy sat down at his desk, put his head in his hand and blew out a lot of air.

"Sheriff, is it safe to say that this is your woman out there?" Said agent Blackmore.

"Yes, and who I thought was my best friend."

"Maybe you need to step back and let us handle this."

Clancy looked up at agent Blackmore," I'm as far back as I'm going to get."

Willie Johnson stuck his head into the office and said," Clancy you better come out here."

"What is it?"

"Thom just heard who were looking for. I think he's going to lose it."

"Bring him in here."

Willie came back in with his uncle in tow, sat him down in the chair and said, " Tell the it Sheriff what you just told me."

Thom look like a puppy just Peed on the new rug.

"It's all my fault," said Thom   .

"How so?" Asked agent Blackmore.

"I told Mike about the drugs and the money."

"Maybe you started the beginning." Said Clancy.

"I got to know some of the guys from the farm hanging out at Rollie's. I get a Harley you know they get to drink and they get to brag and told me all about how they're running drugs up from Texas to all the big cities in the Midwest. This is my town to you know. Didn't like all these drugs coming through my town. So I told Mike about it. He told me to get inside the group and see what I could learn.

One night after a pretty big party, or on the Fourth of July. I overheard Jake telling some guy named Matt something that they had enough money to take care of them forever.

Seems Jake and Jimmy has been skimming from the hual for years. They were just mules. Someone else on the drugs."

"When you put Jimmy away, Jake got sloppy. Started to skim more and more off the top. Mike told me not to worry. Said he was taking care of it. Said he knew who owned the drugs and if I stayed inside for a while longer I could help take down someone big."

"Was a Sheriff's Department informed of this?" Asked Blackmore.

"No." Was all Clancy said." Go on."

"Did come here from St. Paul Minnesota. Someone had tried to kill Jimmy there when the fat farm became available to them, they moved here. Jimmy always swore there was a hit on after you after you put him away and Jake took over things went south fast. Jimmy always took care of the money, Jake ran the mules. With Jimmy gone there was no one to control Jake. I get the feeling that when Jake came back from the Black Hills with a woman calling herself 'his wife' well most of the guys were shocked, she's a real looker right Will."

Will Johnson was busy looking at the wall.

"Well anyways, most of the guys that she was way out of his league, she told everyone she was from Detroit, but I heard her on the phone out at Rollie's talking to someone from New Jersey. When her two friends showed up, things got ugly. They started pushing people around and asking a whole Lotta questions. Didn't sit well with Jake."

"So we've got the County attorney withholding information on a major drug operation from the sheriffs department." Said Blackmore.

"Tom, do you know the connection between Mike and Marinelli. asked Clancy.

"Sort of, but I do know he had a thing for Jake's wife."

"What?" Snapped Willie. "When?"

"Years ago, when he was in college."

"How do you know this?" Asked Blackmore.

"He told me, kind of bragging."

"Do you know if there was any contact after she got here?" Asked Clancy.

"I don't know, maybe, I know they were both gone at the same time about a month ago."

"I remember that." Said Clancy. "Mike went to St. Louis for three days. Will, how did you hook up with her?"

"At Rollie's, came on to me. The Jake was the biggest pig she never laid eyes on. Since you wanted a real man. Not looking to fall in love, just get laid?"

Clancy gave will a long walk. Will just stood there looking down at the floor as something unsaid pass between.

"So Mike knew Mary Beth Marinelli, he may knew about her father's business." Said Clancy.

You can be assured of that." Said the FBI agent." If Mike Billings knew Mary Elizabeth Marinelli, it's a good bet he knows what's what."

"So he finds out that the Turner's are running drugs and stealing my money he calls his old girlfriend whose daddy is connected. Daddy sends his guys out here posing as lawyers for the window company."

"Which gives them access to the Turner farm," said Agent Blackmore.

"Then he sends his own daughter after Jake."

"Now that's just creepy." Said Will.

"How did she know he was going to go to the Black Hills?"

"That would be my doing," said Thom. "I was supposed to go with them, but at the last minute there was a problem at the farm. Mike knew that we were all going to the rally."

"Mike tells Marinelli, Jakes going to the bike rally."

"She hooks up with him there, fucks his brains out and ends up in McAbee."

"What about Webster?" Asked Blackmore.

"He gave us his resume, Mike said he would do the background check."

"Then the two shooters show up as friends of Mary Beth."

"So what we got," said Clancy." Ms. Inside, Mary Beth. Mr. police man, the Maccabee County district attorney, the two guys from muscle, at least we forget the door factory attorneys."

"Here's a question. Was it Marinelli's dope, or was he just looking for a quick score?" Asked Will "Maybe just muscling in on the traffic."

"That to."

"Ryan." Was all he said.

"Sheriff, is this Wilkins over at the clinic."

"Hows Bes?"

"Needs stitches over her I, and has a broken collarbone. Other than that not bad, more blood than damage."

"Did she say anything?"

"Said Mike came home acting crazy, yelling knocking things over, talking about how the doctor and how she had ruined everything."

"How did Dr. Whitmore ruin what?"lancy said. He was at a loss. Billings was blaming Rebecca for everything goneing bad . What went bad?

"Sheriff?"

"Yea?"

"Mrs. billing said that he hit her when she tried to call you. She said he started to scream at her, saying she was always your girl."

"OH shit, get which can, and stay put."

"10-4 Sheriff."

"Old jealousies." Said Will." I remember how she would follow you around, but you never knocked on the door."

"She was my sister's best friend. Did you suddenly forget the best friend rule?"

"No, I clearly remember that one."

Chapter 77

Rebecca felt like she was waking up from a bad dream but couldn't get a grip on it she knew she was moving but not how or where he was in the car in the trunk she thought little by little she was coming around Mike Billings, shootings, drugs, could not figure out why?

Chapter 78

"Hilo 1 to County 1, come in."

"County 1 here."

"We got your boy north on Route 4, about 20 miles   outfrom town."

" Can you stay with them?"

"Sure can, We're run quiet mode so he won't know we're here."

"10-4," said Clancy. "Junior get that out to all the police personnel. Get all the civilians off the road."

"Will do Sheriff."

The dispatcher stuck her head in the door and said, "Capt. Andrews is outside with some of his men."

"The Calvary," said Clancy. " Let's go "

Outside, the SWAT captain inform his men were waiting.

"Hey Capt., didn't expect to see you so soon."

"Yeah well we are in the area, called in to get an update Deputy Thomas filled me in on your progress."

"As things are going were probably going to need you."

"Anything you need Sheriff you saved my ass out there at the farm."

"Trust me Capt., I was saving my own ass out there. Thought you should just come along.

"Well, I'm still breathing and I'm here to help."

"Thanks, I'll remember this."

"Sheriff," called his chief deputy. "As a call for you."

"Who is it?"

"Don't know, wouldn't say. Might be important though."

"Okay I'm coming."

Inside he took the phone, and said," this is Sheriff Ryan."

"Good evening Sheriff," came a very feminine voice." My name is Tamra Whitmore. I've been trying to find my daughter Rebecca. It seems everybody I've talked to has told me I need to speak with you."

Clancy was speechless, what can you tell this woman.' High, I'm going to be your new son-in-law. Rebecca's been kidnapped by a murderer who used to be my best friend.'

"Yes Mrs. Whitmore, I don't know how else to tell you this, so I'll be blunt. We believe Rebecca has been kidnapped."

"Oh my God, by whom?"

"Were not absolutely sure, but were about to go get him."

"Sheriff, Rebecca is a well, she's just recovered from a," her voice trailed off.

"I know all about the mugging Mrs. Whitmore."

"Really, Rebecca told you."

"We've talked about a lot of things."

"Sheriff, I'm getting the feeling that you're scared for my daughter."

"Yes ma'am I am."

"What are you telling me Sheriff?"

"She was probably taken because of me by a man I thought was my best friend."

"Because of you, what do you mean?"

"This is very hard for me to put into words, but believe me. Nothing is more as soon as possible important to me on a personal level, to get your daughter back safe and sound."

"I'm never been very good at reading between the lines Sheriff Ryan, so why don't you just tell me straight out?"

"I'm in love with your daughter."

"And."

"She's in love with me."

"Really, how long have you known her?"

"Five days."

"Five," she said, almost choking on the words.

"Please Mrs. Whitmore, this isn't how I envisioned this. I'm in the middle of a major effortto find your daughter, and I will. So please let me get her back, then this will be a whole lot easier to explain."

"Sheriff, what is your first name?"

"Clancy."

"May I call you Clancy?"

"Of course."

"Well Clancy I'm a little taken aback here. You're saying that you fell in love with Rebecca in just five days?"

"No ma'am, it was closer to two days."

"Two days?" Said Mrs. Whitmore.

"Mrs. Whitmore, Rebecca is the most amazing woman I've ever known. Two days or two years won't change that."

Well Clancy, all I can say is, go get her back. I'll be coming to McAbee on Friday We can talk more than. Please find her,"

"Yes ma'am I intend to."

"Thank you Clancy. Goodbye for now."

When Clancy hung up the phone his hands were shaking. "That was rough," he thought. "Not the best way to make a first impression."

"Hank," yelled Clancy.

"Yes Sheriff?"

"Let's go get this mutt."

Hank saw the steely resolve on the face of the Sheriff. After five years as a Maccabee County deputy, he'd never seen that kind of look in Clancy's eyes.

Chapter 79

Rebecca was awake now. She did make a sound for fear of being put under again.

Where they were She didn't know how long they'd been driving, or where they were.

After a while the truck slowed, keeping down the road as if looking for something. Without warning, the truck turned onto a small dirt road covered overwith brush. Rebecca could hear the bushes scraping against the sides of the truck as they moved forward.

They finally came to a stop.

"Get up I know you're awake."

"Why you doing this Mike? What did I ever do to you?"

"You showed up, now walk."

"I can't see."

"I don't care, walk."

Chapter 80

"Hilo one to County one, over."

"County one, go."

"We've got the suspect stopped in the woods to clicks north of I 76 off route 4."

"10-4," said Clancy." What's up there Hank?"

"Isn't that the old limestone quarry?"

"Yeah, what the hell is he doing up there?"

"County one to Hilo one. Maintain surveillance, were on our way."

Chapter 81

"Where are we going to?" demanded Rebecca.

"Shut the fuck up." Said Mike, in a voice that was trying very hard to sound hard.

"Just walk."

He was pushing her ahead of him. She couldn't see a thing. They came to a clearing set apart from a run down shack.

"Over here, by the house."

The letter around to the far side of the shack where an old beat to shit pickup sat.

"Get in."

"Why should I?"

"I don't want to, but I'll shoot you where you stand you don't get into the fuching truck."

"Shoot me, why would you shoot me?"

"Just do it."

Rebecca didn't believe he would shoot her, but she got in the truck.

" So where are we going?"

"St. Louis."

Chapter 82

"County one Helo one. What your status?"

"On station waiting. No new movement."

Clancy turned to agent Blackmore. "What do you think?"

"This man is not a career criminal. The be thinking in prime time."

"Prime time?"

"Things he seen on TV."

"Helo one come in."

"Helo one."

"Any sign of a second vehicle?"

"Negative sir, we can't see beyond the shack. Too much overgrowth."

"10-4, we're 10 out."

Chapter 83

Rebecca grudgingly got into the truck. Mike reached into his pocket and pulled out the can of ether.

"No, you don't have to do that."

"Hold still and shut up."

Rebecca kicked out, catching Mike square in the jaw. He stumbled but he didn't go down.

"Fucking bitch," he yelled at the cameat her.

He was mad now, shoving her back into the pickup he grabbed the front of her. shirt and slapped her hard three times. He he pulled the rag pocket out of his pocket and smothered her with it.

Chapter 84

"Hilo one, light up the whole area."

"10-4," came the responseas the helo turned on every spotlight it had. Clancy, Agent Blackmore and Capt. Andrews along with two dozen local, state, and federal law enforcement officers poured down the dirt road.

Chapter 85

Half a mile away rusted pickup truck was driving down an access roadthat skirted the quarry. Mike saw the Hilo light up. He knew how close he had been to getting caught. He hadn't counted on a helicopter. He knew he had to get to the main road before he was spotted.

Chapter 86

"They're going Clancy." Said Hank.

"Son of a bitch," yelled Clancy. "Hilo one, they're either on foot or they had another car. Run a search pattern around the quarry, out towards the highway."

"10-4 Sheriff."

"All cars maintain the perimeter of the quarry area. Nobody gets past us tonight."

Chapter 87

Billing saw the Hilo breakoff. It was heading right for him. As of now he was overly exposed if he could make it to the trees he thought he'd have a chance. He was running slow to avoid turning on his lights, but he had to make the trees. He was close, another thousand feet and he be under the canopyof the trees. He began to speed up not a good but getting caught was not a good idea either he thought.

With less than 75 feet to go the truck hit a rut and stopped dead. Overhead the chopper was closing fast, coming up to the access road.

"Shit," he screamed. He rocked the truck back and forth until he finally got it free and raced for the woods.

Chapter 88

In the chopper agent Rodriguez and Deputy Stone were scanning the area with night vision goggles when Stone said, "over there, what's that?"

"Where?" Said Rodriguez.

"At the end of that dirt road that heads into the woods. I saw somethin.'"

Rodriguez tapped the pilot on the shoulder and pointed at the place where the road when into the trees.

Chapter 89

Billings had made it into the trees, but the chapter had turned right on his tail within seconds. He was sure he'd been seen. He stopped the truck under some thick brush as the chopper flew past.

Panic began to seep into Billings thoughts. He couldn't get caught, so much to lose.

He began to drive faster. If he got to the interstate he'd be home free he was driving much faster now, just missing a stump. The highway was close now, 'down this hill and I here.' He thought. But where was the chopper?

As he approached the blacktop he slowed to a stop and waited. Nothing passed by, still he waited. Finally he get out of the truck and crept down to the road, looking both ways several times. Now he was sure he was going to make it.

Chapter 90

"Hilo one, one of you got?"

"Movement, North by Northwest of your position.'

"What kind of movement?"

"Not sure, but there's something on the access road under the tree canopy."

Clancy thought about where they were. He knew these woods fairly well. The old quarry was where they would go to drink beer and Park with their girlfriends. Sort of a 'Lovers Lane.

"Hilo one, north of your point is Bottom Creek Road. If he's headed that way he's making for the interstate."

"Copy that, We'll be watching the road."

Chapter 91

Billings was still unable to drive out onto the blacktop. Fear was setting in, starting to get to him. Is about to head out in the chopper came in low over the road.

Billing set still. Soon enough he was going to have to move. The be coming up from behind soon enough. He waited them in a fit of impatience, drove out onto the road turn left and began heading towards I-76.

Chapter 92

"We got a truck westbound on bottom Creek Road. An old one, rusted through

"10-4, all cars NW. Bottom Creek Rd.. Suspect heading towards I-76."

Chapter 93

Mike Billings had been driving for about a mile, thinking he was going to make it, when the whole road lit up like it was daylight.

"Person in the pickup. Stop your vehicle and pull to the side." Came a voice Billings instantly recognized.

"Junior."

"God dammit, God dammit, God damn them." Billing screamed as he beat the steering wheel. He didn't know where to go, he had to lose the chopper. He had to find a place to hide or he could the cop or the chopper couldn't go. He knew of a place, so more quiet where he could think. If you could just get to the road he knew where to go.

Chapter 94

Clancy and Blackmore were leading the parade of police cars and vans down the small Bobby access road heading to where the chopper had last seen movement.

"We don't even know if it's him in that truck," said Clancy. "Could be anybody?"

"Maybe?" Said agent Blackmore." But I doubt it. This is the only way that makes any sense."

"Yeah, Mike was never the outdoorsy type. He's not dragging Rebecca through the woods."

"County one Hilo."

"Go ahead Sheriff."

"You got this truck?"

"Yeah, westbound on Road six. Doing about 75 miles an hour. Ignored are called to stop."

"Got to be him." Said Blackmore.

"Hilo one. Stay with them, and keep us up-to-date."

"10-4 Sheriff."

Chapter 95

Billings knew the chopper was right above them. If he could get to Knoll, he could lose them in the trees. The Woods, as it was called, as it was called was laced with backcountry roads under heavy trees and brush. If you knew your way around, and Mike did, you could get lost in there for days.

He needed to get from route 4 and then to 6 East. Timing was critical . He pulled into a grove of thick trees and slammed on his brakes. Just as the he had hoped, the chopper flew past. Billings made a hard left drove up an overgrown dirt road it was gone.

Chapter 96

"Hilo one to County one, we lost him."

"What?" Yelled Clancy. "How could you lose him?"

"We had him. He turned into the woods."

"Where?"

"Route 6, about a mile east of 4."

"Knoll Woods." Said Clancy as he slammed his hand into the dash.

Hank Brown's voice came over the radio, "units three and nine, get over to route 30 near the state park. Unit 5 Work Your Way up and down 6. Unit 4 do the same on route 4."

All cars answered.

"County two to County one."

"Go to."

"If he's in Knoll Woods, were not going to have enough people to cover all the exits."

"I know."

"Hilo want to County one. We got about 20 more minutes to have to break off for fuel."

Clancy was getting madder," by the minute this just keeps getting better as we go."

The radio crackled with the voice of Deputy Thomas, "Sheriff I got over 30 people here, with at least two dozen cars and trucks. They all showed up wanting to help."

"Do it, surround Knoll woods. You know the area, do it."

"What about my dogs?"

"Bring them."

Anybody listening to the police radio, could hear the harshness in Clancy Ryan's voice. Everyone also knew there'd be a price to pay for it. "Hilo one, sweep the perimeter until you have to go for fuel."

Chapter 97

Rebecca was wide awake now. She had a terrific had a headache probably due to all the ether and being slapped around by Billings. She could feel her face staying.

Unable to move she lay quietly in the backseat. She could feel the rough road under the truck, so she assumed they were still in the woods it was so dark, no lights at all. Her mouth was dry she had to Pee.

"I got a pee." She finally said.

"Tough shit." Snarled Mike.

"Come on I got to go."

"So go. What makes you think I give a shit?"

"What the hell is wrong with you. Have you gone completely off your rocker?"

"I've never felt better my entire life."

Something the way Mike said that, gave Rebecca a chill. Had he really slipped that far from the guy she met not five days ago? What could all this be about?

"Come on Mike I have in my pants as I was three. I really gotta go."

"Jesus Christ, what a crybaby."

"Mike, please."

Billing slammed on the brakes so hard, Rebecca slid down onto the floor, banging your head hard on the phone on the door.

"Get out."

"My hands are tied. How my supposed to pee with my hands tied?"

Bullies pulled on a buck knife and cut the duct tape around her wrists.

"So go."

"What, you gonna watch me pee, is that what this is all about. You want to watch me pee, you get off on that, you sick fuck?" Her eyes were blazing with hatred. She was going to kill this basterd.

"You run, I'll kill you. Got it."

"Yeah, I got it."

Once Mike turned around Rebecca unbuckled her belt, taking sure to make a lot of noise with the buckle. Billings had turned his his back to Rebecca and never saw her come at him. She hit him right above his neck line with rock size of a grapefruit. The effect was immediate down to his knees then pitching forward flat on his face. She was going to hit him again, when he rolled over on his back. He had the buck knife in his hand and was wildly swinging at her.

Rebecca's first thought was to get in the pickup but Mike was getting up. She'd hit them in the right place but she wasn't that strong so she turned and ran straight into the woods.

Chapter 98

"County 9 County one,we got the pickup."

"Where?" Was all Clancy said.

"Quarter-mile off the road, right where the chopper lost it. Off 6 East of 4."

"On our way."

"County 1 to County3."

"Here Sheriff."

"Bring the dogs."

"10-4 almost there now."

Clancy was confused why give up the truck. Billings could have driven around the woods for days. Something else had happened. As mad as Clancy, he was just as scared, scared for the woman he'd only known less than a week, Scared because a week wasn't enough. He had to get her back, just had to.

Chapter 99

As Clancy came up Route six he saw a county squad car parked on the side of the road. Lights flashing, Deputy Parker was standing by a clump of bushes waving his flashlight.

"What do you got Bill?"

"Through the weeds, about a quarter-mile up."

"Who found the pickup?"

"I did sir. Been up this road a few times. You know, before I was married."

Clancy was too mad to smile, but he got what Parker was saying.

"Good work, who's up there?"

"Chief deputy Thomas went up there 10 minutes ago with Will Johnson. Told me to wait here, wait for you."

Two more squads come flying up stopping just short of the hidden road.

"Capt. Andrew should be right behind us. We got cars all around the woods." Said Hank Brown.

"Good." He said. "Stay here with Parker, wait for the SWAT guys. Keep your eyes open and stay together. I don't want him doubling back on you."

"10-4 Sheriff, we can move the cars across the road. That way we can see anyone coming out of the woods," "Good." Then he said to Hank, "let's go."

Chapter 100

Mike Billings have laid on the ground trying to get his bearing. That pitch is really hit him hard and now she was gone. He was about to get into the pickup when he saw lights coming up the road. If he started the truck now they'ed be on him, so he too turned and ran into the woods.

Chapter 101

Clancy, agent Blackmore and Hank Brown found Junior and Willie right where Parker had said they'ed be. Juniors dogs were barking like crazy looking forward to the hunt, "What do you think we have here?"asked Clancy.

"Sheriff, we got fresh blood here, on the ground and on tis rock." said Junior.

Clancy bent down and looked over the scene.

"She had him."

"That's what I was thinking," said Junior. "The dogs are barking up to different trails. One up the road and one went off into the woods. There is blood that way.

"She got away," said Clancy. You could hear the relaxation in his voice, "This is good she ran. Junior take two of your dogs and follow the blood."

Two more deputies that come up he road, Clancy told them to go with Junior.

"We'll take the other two dogs up the road. Willie, come with us. You can handle these dogs right?"

"Sure Clancy, be glad to."

"Then, can you wait here for the rest of the guys, act as a base.?"

Sure, I'll send the SWAT guys after you the blood. Keep me informed as to where you are."

"All right let's go."

Chapter 102

Rebecca was lost, she'd run up the road at first but then thought Mike might be coming after her with the truck. She gone about 100 yards before she ran into the woods. Tired, scared, hungry and now lost.

" How the hell did it come to this," she thought." Lost and alone, in the dark in the middle of nowhere.

Something moved off the left, startling her. As she turned towards the sound, her foot caught in a tree root, twisting it badly and throwing her to the ground. She had to hold her breath to keep from screaming, the pain was so great. Gritting her teeth she sworn her breath.

"What else could happen?" She whispered to herself.

She knew she had to get up, tried and failed, tried again. Failed again. It didn't feel broke and she thought, but she couldn't put any weight on it.

She was bone tired. She was going to have to sleep for a while. Rebecca set down against a tree, and closed her eyes.

Chapter 103

Clancy, Hank and Willie had been going up the road until the dogs pulled them intothe woods.

"Hank stay here, watch the road and keep your flashlight on. Remember, Mike is still out here."

"Got it."

Just as they began to move off the road, a call came on over the radio.

"County 3 to 1."

"Go ahead Junior."

"Dogs lost seant. Our suspect use some type of chemical to cover his tracks."

"Shit." Swore Clancy." Get back to the road and head up this way."

"10-4."

Chapter 104

Voices, Rebecca was sure she heard voices. Close by but where. She screamed.

"Here." Only loud enough for the grass to hear.

"Here." Louder this time but not nearly loud enough, the voices were drifting away.

"Here." She screamed with everything she had left.

Chapter 105

"You hear that?" Said Clancy.

"Yep over there." Said Will.

"Come on, bring the dogs."

They were about 100 feet into the woods, when they heard it again."

"What was that?"

"It's Rebecca." Said Clancy.

"Rebecca." He shouted." Where are you baby?"

"Here." He heard that.

"Where?"

Clancy couldn't pin down where the voice was coming from.

"Where?" He yelled as loud as he could.

What he heard back was weak and faint but sounded so close.

"Here by the big tree." Rebecca whispered.

He saw her, lying on her side next to an old oak tree.

"Here," he yelled." Over here," waving his flashlight that Willie.

Clancy was down on his knees. "Rebecca, baby talk to me."

"Oh hi Clancy, where you been?"

"I'm here now, are you hurt?"

"That just a broken ankle."

Clancy scooped her up in his arms and headed towards the road.

"Get the EMTs up here."

"I need some water."

Rebecca put her arms around him and snuggled into his neck. This man was safe she thought, her man.

Clancy race down the road with Rebecca safely in his arms. No woman on the planet was safer than Rebecca Whitmore was at this moment. She knew it, and she gave herself to it.

End Game

Rebecca slowly woke up to the sound of people talking. At first she thought she was still in the woods, then she remembered Clancy caring her down the road to the ambulance. So who was talking? She opened her eyes and saw her mother sitting on the side of the bed, holding her hand.

"Mom?" She said, still very weak." What are you doing here?"

"Now that's a silly question, where else should I be?" Said Mrs. Whitmore.

"In Boston, with Dad."

"Oh he's here to, just went down for some supper."

"Supper, what time is it?"

"It six it 6 o'clock in the evening. You've been asleep for 16 hours. Dr. said it was an effect of the ether. Nasty stuff to be inhaling, so I'm told."

"How long have you been here?"

"Only about an hour and a half. We left Boston right after I talked to Clancy. Oh honey, that's one good-looking boy you got there "Mother, he is the high Sheriff of the whole county. Show a little respect please."

"And you're going to marry him?"

"Yep, soon as I can."

"Good."

"Good? I thought you'd go nuts when you found out."

"The way he talked last night and the fact that he slept right here on the floor all night, well, he seems like the real deal."

"He is mom. He really slept on the floor?"

"Yes, it wasn't until your father and a man named Will drag him out here was willing to leave.

Rebecca looked around and became a little frightened by the lack of men.

"Don't worry honey, there's enough cops around this billing to start a war. There is a SWAT team down in the lobby, plus, there's a mean -looking deputy with a bandage on his head just down the hall. I swear he almost shot the flower guy."

"That would be Junior."

"Yes, he said he owes you." Said Mrs. Whitmore looking over the top of her herglasses.

"It's a long story Mom, but he means it."

The phone rang, Mrs Whitmore answered it   and   said. "Hello." Pause, and then said, "yes she is." She said hello two more times but never did get an answer.

Clancy Ryan Sheriff Maccabee County Illinois, stormed in the room, fell to his knees took, her hand and said "Hi" "that's it, hi?"

"Couldn't think of anything else to say. I've been so worried."

"I'm fine, really. When can I get out of here?"

"Dr. said tomorrow morning, once the cast sets."

For the first time she looked down at her feet. At her feet under the blanket one side was deftly larger than the other.

"Broken?"

"Yep, in two places."

"Wonderful. What is it with me, do I like a target to you?"

"This was not your fault in any way. You are in the wrong place at the wrong time. There's a whole conspiracy here, been going on for months. And apparently Mike is smack in the middle of."

"Then why kidnap me?"

"We think Mike was trying to get at me."

"Why?"

"We don't know. He beat Bea to a pulp just before he took you."

"Oh God, is she...?"

"Fine, she's beat up, but shall be fine."

"I still don't get it?"

"I do," said Will Johnson as he came in through the door, followed by Rebecca's father.

"Hi Daddy."

"Hi sweetie. You doing okay?"

"Yeah I'm fine."

Clancy turned to will and said, "what do you mean, you know?"

"Been talking with Tom, said Mike was always jealous of us. thought he was only just a tag-a-long."

"That's bull. We always included him."

"I know that, but think about it Clancy. We were always leaving him behind. In high school we played on every team, but he only ran cross-country. Remember when he placed third at the state finals."

"Yeah and were both standing at the finish line there'd hear him on."

"Sure we were, but who did the papers interview that day, Mr. big shot college-bound football player."

"Me"

"Right, and remember the basher twins?"

"Well there were only two of them."

Rebecca hit Clancy in the shoulder.

"Hey."

"Don't you make fun Clancy."

"Better get used to that Clancy. With three brothers a girl's got to learn how to defend yourself."

"All three of her brothers were scared to death of her." Said her dad.

"I'm sorry, so you're saying that all this goes back 20 years?"

"That's what I'm saying. Tom said Mike wanted to get out of here, wanted to go to the big city, even talk to divorcing Bea."

"Divorcing Bea, she adores him."

"In his eyes, he was always the second choice."

"What do you mean, Will?" Asked Rebecca.

"From the fourth grade, Bea only had eyes for Clancy. But he never went there" "The best friend rule."

"Right." Will said sheepishly. "Apparently, that's been a sore spot with him all along."

"Let me get this straight, Mike Billings through his whole life away because he was harboring a long-term jealous streak. That's nuts."

"Seemed little strange to me to." Said will.

"Not so strange, "said Mrs. Whitmore. "We have four children. In our family. Two doctors, a lawyer and our youngest Ben. Ben's been to two colleges and an art school. He has no idea what he's going to do. Rarely talks to his brothers. The only one he'd ever talk to was Rebecca, and she moved away"

"Kids got no metal." Said Rebecca's father, "been babied all his life."

"Still." Said Mrs. Whitmore with hard glance at her husband." He's unable to find his path due to the expectations of his older siblings."

"Been special," said Rebecca." It will just take a little longer for him."

"I hope so." Said her dad.

"Mom, Dad. May I talked a Clancy private."

"Sure honey, we right outside."

Chapter 106

After her parents and Will have left with Clancy was still holding her hand, Rebecca said," Oh Clancy it was so scared. It was like Chicago all over again."

"You're safe now." Said Clancy"I will never let anything happen to you again."

"Promise?"

"With all that I am."

"I'm going to hold you to your promise, Mr. Ryan."

"You weren't the only one who was scared last night. I was so afraid I was going to lose you. I'm so sorry you had to get wrapped up in this."

"Don't worry about me I'm pretty tough after all."

"Never doubted it for a minute."

"What did you tell my parents?"

"The truth, always seem to be the best approach."

"And my mother didn't go nuts?"

"She flew halfway across the country, didn't she?"

"That's normal in my family. They were always there for us. They seem to have accepted our situation, right?"

"I'm sure we'll have some more questions after all this blows over."

"You are going to get?"

"As I breathe."

"Any leads?"

"There was a car stolen this morning, up near Westmore, north of the woods. It's a good bet it was Mike."

"St. Louis."

"What?"

"St. Louis. Just before he put me out, he said they were going to St. Louis."

Clancy stood up and went out to the hall. "Junior, get on the horn to St. Louis PD.

Mike might be heading that way. You got the make and tag number for that sedan that was stolen?"

"Sure to Sheriff."

"Send them everything we got so far. And just for grins, send them up the sheet we got a Mary Beth Marinelli."

"Got,it."

Back at the bedside, Rebecca said. "Can you get me out of here?"

"Don't you think it's a good idea to stay a while?"

"No I don't. I'll go crazy in here."

"Yeah, but you're safe in here."

"I feel like a prisoner."

"I'll talk to the doctor, but no promises."

So on a beautiful September, Clancy wheeled Rebecca out into a perfect sunset evening. It had taken a lot of convincing to get the doctor to agree but Clancy managed. That plus the armed guard escorting the patient to a waiting squad.

As Clancy was helping Rebecca into the truck she leaned into him and said, "I want to go to your house,. No more hiding."

"I already promised the guestroom to your mom and dad."

"Not what I had in mind, I need to hold you tonight."

"That could be a little awkward."

"So what, I'm not a little girl anymore."

"Of that, I am sure." Said Clancy, making Rebecca.

Blush a little"

Mom, Dad, I'm staying at Clancy's tonight to."

"Of course you are where else would you go?"

"I'm really beginning to like her." said Clancy.

"Yeah, and I think she likes you to."

Chapter 107

Back at the house, things started to feel nicer. Clancy cooked steaks on the grill while Rebecca opened a couple of bottles of good wine and all had a chance to settle down. Clancy was amazed at how open and honest Rebecca's parents seemed and how well they got along. Before you knew it the men were downstairs playing with Clancy's theater system talking gators football and the NFL. Mr. Whitmore with a true New England Patriots fan, even a season-ticket holder. Clancy was in fact Chicago Bears Fan.

Once the men were downstairs Rebecca's mother fell quiet.

"What is it mom?"

"He's truly a wonderful man."

"I know that, what is it mom?"

"I had hopes of you coming back to Boston, to stay. It's probably not going to happen now is?"

"I don't see that either. Even after what happened I have a good job, people of been great here and then there's Clancy."

"You really love him don't you?"

"Oh yes, He's more then I could've ever hoped for."

"Well it's a pretty good bet that your fathers taken to him."

"Gator Nation strikes again."

"Oh God will I ever be over."

"I'll bet you solid Penny is going to get worse."

The men came back up from the basement, and began to clear up dinner.

"You have got to see that system Clancy has downstairs, Tammy."

"Boys with their toys," said his wife.

"Yeah but their really cool toys," replied John Whitmore.

Chapter 108

Everyone was laughing feeling good and not worrying about the recent events, when the phone rang.

"Hello Sheriff Ryan," came a smooth feminine voice.

"Yes whom I talking to?"

"Not important right now, What's important is our money."

"What money?"

"Look Ryan, don't go stupid on me."

"You look, whoever you are. I never saw any money, but if you come to my office we can talk about it." He paused, and then said," Mary Elizabeth."

"Not quite the hick Sheriff we thought. Still we are missing a lot of money and we will get it back. You may have thrown a wrench in our plans but nothings changed."

"Everything is changed. Come if you're up to it, I'll be here waiting."

Clancy slammed down the phone," I'm afraid this isn't over yet."

"I never thought it was Clancy," said Rebecca." But will see it through together."

"Not we, me. I won't let you be a target again."

"I was in this from the start and I'll see it finished, my choice." She said.

"Stubborn and beautiful, a deadly combination." Said Clancy.

"Just like her mother." Said John kind of whimsical.

"This is not funny dad. These people have already killed three people." Said Rebecca.

Clancy was quietly sitting, thinking. Finally he reached over and grabbed the phone. "Alice, find Hank Brown for me please."

"He's right here Sheriff."

Hank Brown came on the phone and said," Hello Sheriff. How's Dr. Whitmore doing."

"I think she'll be fine. Hank, I just got a call from Mary Elizabeth Marinelli. She seems to be after the money that the Turner were supposed to to have skimmed."

In all of this, there was never any money."

"I tried to tell her that. Seems to think we have it."

"Don't I wish."

"Get the word out anyone, and I mean anyone, who doesn't fit, I want ID'd. No ID running for vagrancy. I want this county lockdown. First thing in the morning, I want people out of the Turner's farm. Go over it with a fine tooth comb, turn it upside down."

"Got it. "

"Also, get a hold of someone up in Peoria to check on Jimmy Turner and the shooter we got there."

"I'll get right on that. You think they're coming back."

"Yes I do, money makes people crazy, and a lot of money makes people killers."

"I'll get the word out, I'm going to send a car around your place just to watch things."

"Good idea, Use the unmarked squad"

"Low-profile. I'll have it set up about a half a block away."

"Perfect. Maybe they'll slip up."

"10-4." Said Hank and hung up

Chapter 109

After Clancy hung up the phone he turned to Rebecca and her parents," I'm a little worried about you all being here. Maybe it would be safer at the B&B, or maybe back in Boston."

"Now Clancy will be fine, what could ever happen." Said Tammy.

Clancy stood up and pointed at the two bullet holes in the front door frame.

"We've already been shot at once this week. They know where I live."

"Oh my word," Said Tammy. "Was anybody hurt?"

"No thank God. Still, I will not risk it any of you."

Clancy sought for a moment, I've got it then said, "I got it." As he grabbed for his phone.

"Hi it's me. I need a huge favor from you. I'm hoping that I can put Rebecca's parents in your guestroom. I'm afraid I might still be a target until this thing is over. Okay, great. I'll bring them over after dark. "

"I'm not leaving," said Rebecca with her hands on her hips.

"I only want your folks out of harm's way. That was my mother. She's willing to put them up in her guestroom, sounded to me like she was looking forward to it."

"I don't know Clancy," said John. "We don't want to leave you to out on a limb."

"It's your call, but I think you be safer at my mother's house. It's only three blocks away."

"Well I for one will go." Tammy said. "I would love to meet your mother Clancy. We have so many things to talk about."

"It's settled then." Said Clancy. Looking at Rebecca's father, he asked," John?"

"She speaks, I follow."

"Great. Let's go out the back in through the yard behind us. My mother's house is three blocks north of the next intersection. It's dark enough so no one will see us."

"Why all the speaking around?" Asked Tammy.

Clancy pointed that the two bullet holes and said," In case somebody's watching.

Been shot at once already this week. Let's go."

"Are we forgetting something?" Said Rebecca pointing to her knee high cast.

"Sorry honey sure did. Okay let's go for a ride in the S.S."

"S.S? Asked John.

"65 Malibu S.S. Convertible," said Rebecca." I got to drive it."

"By all means. Let's go for a ride." Said John.

"Once a motorhead, always a motorhead," said Tammy.

"Absolutely." Said Tammy and her father wat exactly the same moment.

"He's also got a 71 Hurst Olds 442 convertible and a complete, although apart, '63 California fuelly Corvette convertible."

"Fuelly, '63 fuelly? 327 porcupine?"

"Y were going to rebuild."

"Can I help?" Asked John.

"Sure but it's going to take years to get it right."

"Oh God, take me now." Said Tammy.

Clancy was bending down to pick Rebecca up when an explosion rocked the house and blew out his brand-new picture window.

"Down, down on the floor," yelled Clancy as he grabbed his done and headed for the front door.

"No Clancy, no, stop," yelled Rebecca. But it was too late. Clancy was hell bent for the front door. So Rebecca did the only thing she could think of. She stuck out her cast and tripped him. He fell flat on his face just as the door splintered apart in a hail of gunfire. The phone rang.

Clancy dragged himself over to the phone, grimaced at Rebecca and said, "That hurt."

"Not as much as those bullets would've."

"Point taken," he said as he reached for the phone.

"What?"

"Well Sheriff, do we have your attention now?"

"You sure do motherfucher, right up to the point when I bury you."

"Now, now Sheriff, all we want his arm what's ours."

"How many times do I have to tell you, we don't have your money."

"Oh how I wish I could believe you?"

"You should ask Mike Billings. He's the one missing."

"Missing for you. I know right where he is. But don't worry, he won't be needing any money anymore."

"What the fuck does that me?"

"Figure it out."

"Look bitch, I'll find you. I'm going to hunt you down, and when I do..."

"What tough guy you gonna kill me. Bet that'll get you reelected Clancy could hear sirens screaming in the distance.

"Gotta go now Mary. Got company coming over."

Chapter 110

Clancy slammed the phone down as sounds as the fire department came roaring up to the house. Clancy looked out for the first time and saw his brand-new County Tahoe going up in flames.

"Aw man, I like the truck."

Hank Brown came running up the walk. "Everybody okay anybody hurt but the fuck happened?"

Clancy had never heard Hank Brown swear before," I'm going to tell your mother, Hank."

"Sorry, who did this? Was it the Marinelli people?"

"Yeah, I got a call from Mary Elizabeth right after. Wants her money."

Hank threw his hands up and said, " What money?"

"The money that the Turners skimmed off the top of the drugs they were running."

"Well it's good to know they don't have it."

"What do you mean?"

"This whole thing has been about that money. They still don't have. If it really exists who has.

"Stay with the plan to search the Turner farm. I'll call Agent Blackmore in Chicago first thing in the morning, See if I can get his team back out here. Got to be something out there we missed. Did you call the hospital?"

"Yeah. Both awake both under heavy guard."

"Good, once you get the search going, were going to talk to both of them."

"I'm so sorry I got you all involved in this. It's not what this county is about."

"None of this is your fault Clancy," said Rebecca." Why are they coming at you?"

"They think we've taken the drug money and they wanted back."

"What if they knew the sheriffs department had the money, why would they think you'd give it back?" Said John.

"Sheriff, they know it hasn't been put into the evidence locker," said Hank." So they must think were Heidi did on them."

"Maybe. I think they're closer than we think."

"Another rat?"

"Yeah, could be."

Clancy was getting madder by the minute. This was slowly getting away from him. He wished he knew what the hell was going to happen next. He knew we had to do something, he just wasn't sure what.

"Hank, see that Dr. and Mrs. Whitmore get over to my mother's house. Then come right back."

"Got it."

"I got in the idea that maybe we can flush these mutts out."

"Clancy, we don't feel right leaving you here like this," said John.

"I know, but I'd feel a lot better knowing that you are out of line of fire."

"Still, it doesn't seem right."

"You were me please."

Chapter 111

After Rebecca's parents had been taken to Clancy's mother's house and Hank had come back, Clancy outlined his plan"

"Just might work Sheriff."

"Just might."

"We're gonna need the FBI."

"I'm calling Blackmore first thing in the morning."

"You think we need to swat people guys to."

"Yeah but not right away. "Get out to the farm at first light. Take 3 or 4 deputies. I'll be out around 10 o'clock. By then I should have it all in place."

Chapter 112

After Hank had left, Clancy looked around his house. His door was busted, the windows busted again and he was no closer to the truth. At least he still had Rebecca. But where was she?

"Rebecca," he called out. When he got no response."

He called out again. " Rebecca?"

Still no answer. He began to run around the house. Downstairs, out into the yard. He finally found her asleep upstairs in the bedroom. My God she was beautiful. He stood and stared for a long time before and going back downstairs.

Chapter 113

Hank and his group made it out to the farm by 6 AM. ATF had gone over the bomb site thoroughly and found no trace of drugs, just as Thom had said. Hank now thought the trailer was meant to lure them in and blow them up. Not a cheery thought, though it did make Hank more resolute to get these bastered.

They started with the house, making sure there are no more booby-traps. They looked in every corner and open every drawer. Hank had to debt guys going over the barns and all the other out buildings.

By the time Clancy showed up, Hank and his crew had been over the property twice. No money, no drugs and especially, no explosives.

"Anything?" Asked Clancy.

"No." Was all Hank said.

"Okay phaze two."

Clancy open the trunk of his replacement squad and pulled out two large suitcases and took them inside. Clancy and Hank both assumed they were being watched and hoped their little ruse would start the ball rolling.

After a half an hour of sitting around inside, Clancy and Hank each carried one suitcase out to the squads. Two of the deputy stood with their shotguns at the ready. Clancy and Hank each lifted their case as if it was heavier than before.

"Okay all of us, in a line, back to the station."

First went Hank, followed by Clancy than the two deputy cars.

They did not leave unseen.

The line of four cars raced to the county right into town up to the courthouse.

There they rushed inside with the cases. They took the cases into the evidence room which had several lockers that were steel reinforced were Clancy put to two steel hard locks on the doors.

"If someone was going to break into the lockers," said Clancy." They're gonna need a blowtorch. That should keep it safe"

The last bit he announced loud enough for everyone to hear.

"What's in there?" Asked the deputy on duty.

"Can't say right now." Said Clancy.

Quietly said to Hank," If we still got a mole this should flush them out."

"Sheriff," called Alice the dispatcher." We got a hit on the guy you got up in Peoria."

"And"

"Names Alberto Fornellie From, what a surprise, Trenton, New Jersey.

"Priors"

"Boat loads, strong-arm, , drugs, theft, nice little list.'

"Call Judge Pennybrook. Tell him what we've got and make an appointment for me this afternoon. Call the states attorneys office in Springfield and get someone down here fast. We need to have all our ducks in a row real soon."

As Clancy was reading over Fornellie's rap sheet, his private line began to ring.

"Sheriff Ryan."

"Was that little bit of theater for my benefit?"

"Just taking care of the county's property, Ms. Marinelli."

"You mean my property don't you?"

"On the contrary, it's evidence in a series of crimes against the people of Maccabee County Illinois."

"We don't have to be enemies Clancy."

"I think we do.,Marinelli."

"There is enough for both of us."

"Keep talking."

Maybe we can come to an agreement?"

"Or maybe I'll just keep it all."

"That would be a bad idea."

"You blew up my truck. I likeDE that truck."

"That money could buy you 10 trucks."

"Let me think about."

"Don't think too long. If we can come to some kind of agreement, I want you to release deputy Webster."

"That's going to be hard to do."

"Why's that?"

"Because you're all college boyfriend put a bullet through his brain yesterday afternoon. I'm surprised you didn't know this."

Clancy heard what was a series of soft gas, almost like a sob.

"Ms. Marinelli you still there?"

"I... I can't talk, I, I'll call you back."

"One more thing, Miss Marinelli, I'll do no deal unless I get Mike Billings back live.'

"That may not be possible."

Mary Elizabeth Marinelli's voice choked as she spoke. It made Clancy wondered just who Deputy Webster really was.

"Nonetheless, it is nonnegotiable."

"I'll call you back," came a voice that sounded almost broken.

After Clancy hung up the phone, he walked across the hall to the empty office where agents Blackmoore and Rodriguez were sitting in front of several computer monitor.

"You got it?'

"Yep, good imprint. Stand up in any court."

"Now we wait."

"Sheriff, just for the record. That suitcase trick was pretty lame."

"Best I could do on a short notice," said Clancy." With any luck she'll have bought into it."

"She's smart, but did you hear the sound of her voice when she heard about Webster?"

"Yeah, our staff stress needles went off the charts."

"What's that about?"

"Don't know, do we even have an idea who he was."

"Alice." Called Clancy.

"Did we get anything back on Deputy Webster's prints?"

"Not that I've seen."

"Send it again. Tell him we needed ASAP."

"Will do Sheriff."

Clancy's phone rang again only this time it was Rebecca.

"I'm going nuts."

"Short trip."

"Very funny, I feel like I'm under house arrest."

"Think of it as protective custody."

"You're joking, right. That's supposed to be funny, right?"

"I thought so."

"I'm going to kick youra..."

"Careful there Whitmore. You can't go around threatening the sheriff."

"Fine."

"I'll be home in about 10 minutes, how about lunch at Millie's?"

"Can't. Our collective mothers are taking me out to lunch. Seems they're getting along famously.

"Not without an escort. I'm sending the deputy overdrive you."

"Come on Clancy it's just lunch."

I can always have you arrested for attacking a police officer."

"What attack?"

"You kicked me last night, with your cast."

"Boneheaded, hard assed, Irish rat bastered. I was saving your sorry ass."

"My, my, my. Such language. They didn't teach you that finishing school. Okay, have your lunch. But remember, there are still people out there that will hurt you."

"Thank you." She said in her best finishing school voice." Mother will be so pleased."

After Rebecca had hung up, Clancy called who Alice. "Send a squad around to pick up my mother and Mrs. Whitmore. Then send the car around to pick up Rebecca and take them to Millie's."

After that he picked up his phone and dialed his mothers number.

"Hello." Said his mother.

"Hi mom, I hear you're going to lunch today."

"Yes dear, Tammy and I are going to be fast friends. She is a lovely woman."

"That's great mom. Look, I just talked to Rebecca and she thinks it would be safer if I send the deputy over to pick you all up."

"Do you think that's necessary dear?"

"I don't but Rebecca is still a little skittish about things"

"Well okay, if you think it's necessary."

"If you think it's necessary?" Better safe than sorry always say.

Alice stuck her head around the corner after he hung up the phone and said, "Clancy Ryan you going to burn in hell for that one."

"I'm sure I'll hear about it, but I'd face the wrath of God himself to protect those ladies, and tell the deputy not to take no for an answer."

"Okay you're the boss."

Chapter 114

"Clancy," called agent Blackmore.

"Yeah," said Clancy as he stuck his head back into the little room.

We've been thinking. With Webster dead and Billings run off, Marinelli isn't a getting good Intel. She didn't know about Webster because Billings didn't tell her. Were thinking your department is most likely clean now."

"I sure hope so. I'm getting tired of looking over my shoulder a guys I've known for years."

Clancy's private line rang.

" Sheriff Ryan."

"Do you have a deal?"

"That really depends on you Miss Marinelli. I need to know Mike Billings is part of the deal."

"You'll get him."

"Alive?"

"Yes, alive."

"Now let's talk percentages. I figure I'm good for 70%."

"What, are you nuts?"

"That's what I'm willing to give you to go away. I also need a fall guy to pin the three murders on."

"Three murders?"

"Yep, three."

"Who else?"

"One of the two guys that came to town posing as bikers."

"You got a name?"

"Not on the dead one. We got a guy named Alberto Fratelli, he still alive. We're think that Billings shot the other guy to."

Clancy heard the same gasping voice that he had heard before.

"Ms. Marinelli, what aren't you telling me. The it's time to come clean this is going to work."

"His name was Santos Fratelli, Alberto's brother."

" Why would Billings try to kill these two guys?"

"I don't l, they work for Billings."

She was lying and Clancy could hear it in her voice.

"Okay Ms. Marinelli, when you want to tell me the truth call me back."

Before she could answer he hung up the phone. Across the hall Dan Blackmore shouted, "She was lying about Webster."

"Yeah I got that. Women like her don't cry over a nobody."

"30%, that she piss her off."

"Yeah mad make stupid."

"My guess is Billings should be damn lucky that you want him back."

"It would seem so. He's already killedywo of her team and it's my guess they were, at lest, friends."

Clancy knew she called back, so they were just going to wait.

Chapter 115

Squad car Clancy had sent to pick up Rebecca and the mothers, pulled in the Clancy's driveway. Rebecca was waiting for her future mother-in-law to pick her up, saw the squad and frowned.

"What's this?" She said as the deputy came to the door.

"The sheriff told me to pick you up and take you all to Millie's."

"I told him I didn't need an escort."

"Just doing what I was told, Ms. Whitmore."

"Fine."She said, a little too sharply.

As The deputy helped her down the front stairs and was almost to the squad car when a black van raced up onto the lawn. Two men dressed in black, wearing ski masks jumped out and pointed guns at the startled people. The deputy went for his gun but wasn't quick enough.

"I wouldn't if I were you sonny." Said the first man.

"The second man pointed his gun at Rebecca and said." You'll be coming with us, ma'am."

"The hell I will."

"Get in the truck or I'll kill the deputy right here."

When Rebecca hesitated, the man cocked his pistol and pointed that the deputy. In a flash the man pointing the gun at the deputy, dropped to his knees and fell face first in the grass. From both sides of Clancy's house and on all sides came 10 heavily armed men in full combat gear.

"On the ground now," shouted the lead man." On the fucking ground you piece of shit."

The man through his gun away and got to his knees. One of the men from the SWAT team kicked the man in the back of his head pushing him onto his face.

"Are you okay Dr. Whitmore?" asked Capt. Andrews.

"What the hell just happened?" Asked Rebecca, somewhat stunned.

"I think we just prevented these two assholes from kidnapping you."

"How did you know? Where did you come from?"

"Sheriff Ryan asked if we keep an eye on you. He couldn't figure out why Billings would've taken you unless you were meant to be a bargaining chip if things went south. So he asked us to watch you."

"And where was he going to tell me about this?"

"You have to talk to him about that ma'am."

"Oh I will, you can count on that.

"Deputy, you can take Dr. Whitmore to her luncheon date now."

"Deputy, could you take me by the court house first. I have some business there."

Chapter 116

Clancy had just gotten the phone off the phone with Capt. Andrews, when the squad car carrying Rebecca pulled up outside.

"Here we go." Said Clancy under his breath, as he got up to meet her at the door.

"Hi honey, thought you were going to lunch?"

"Don't you honey me, Clancy Ryan."

"What ever is the matter?"

"You know damn well what's the matter. You had me set up like a piece of bait."

"Yeah so?"

Rebecca was getting madder by the minute.

"Don't you make light of this. Can't you see how upset I am?"

"Oh, I see that. I just don't know why."

"Don't you?"

"Calm down, I told you something could happen. Why do you think I wanted the deputy to drive you? You were drug, bound and dragged all over the county. If I can't protect the woman I love that I should just turn in my badge."

"But..."

"But nothing, where would you be right now if I hadn't sent the captain and his men to watch over you."

"I, I oh shit, I hate losing a good argument."

"And I hate having them."

"I'm sorry Clancy, so on edge lately."

"With good reason."

"Yeah, but I'm not coping so well right now."

"I don't know how you could."

Rebecca reached out for Clancy," just told me a minute."

Clancy took her in his arms, she was shaking, as the tough front she'd been hiding behind crumbled.

"Nobody expects you to be so tough, especially on yourself."

"I'm not tough, I only fool people into thinking I'm tough."

"Who cares what people think."

"I have to care. People expect me to be strong, People need to lean on their doctors. I have to be there for them."

"For right now what's preventing you from being a good doctor."

"Rebecca knew there was nothing.

"I'm just being silly."

"Yeah but you're so damn cute when you are."

Rebecca hit Clancy right in the middle of his chest.

"Now you're under arrest."

"Sure, I could spend the night in jail. I'd be safe there."

"That's not funny."

"Wasn't meant to be."

Clancy knew she was just venting off some of the steam the last couple of days and built up.

"Why don't you go to your luncheon date? I'm sure our mothers are wondering where you went to."

"I don't feel like lunch what I would like is for you to come home with me and cuddle up out under the covers."

"Lunch with mothers, then covers."

Rebecca gave Clancy a look that almost made him reconsider, but in the end he had work to do.

"Deputy, take Dr. Whitmore to my mother's house, and then on to Millie's. Stay with them."

"10-4 Sheriff."

Chapter 117

After the car pulled off Clancy turned to find Will Johnson standing behind him.

"Geez Clancy, you've got it bad."

"So," said Clancy defiantly.

"No man, it's a good thing."

"Can I help you with something,... Martha?"

"No, it's what I can do for you."

"Which is?"

"Farm told me that Jake hit the bank every two weeks like clockwork. Paid his bills and bought supplies with cash. You know Becky Ray over at the bank right. Tells me that Jake had a safety deposit box, a big one. Said he went into it every time he came to town."

"Becky Ray, isn't she about 20 years old?"

"There you go again, always thinking the worst about me."

"Well, once a dog."

"You get a hold that thing with Letty against me for the rest of my life?"

"Yep, that thing is a name. You remember your son, Jack."

Clancy shrugged his shoulders turned and started to walk away.

"Clancy wait."

"What for?" Said Clancy still walking.

"I need to know what to do."

"About what?"

"About Jack. He really doesn't know me."

"Probably a good thing."

"Ask you so for some real help here. She's your sister."

"Call Leddy. Tell her feel a need to connect with Jack. See if he'll even talk to you. Start there."

"Think she'll even talk to me?"

"I will.'

"I will. What about Jack, will he talk to me?"

"Leddy wanted Jack to call Scott dad, Jack refused. Said he only wanted one dead. That says something."

"Okay, thanks Clancy."

"Thank me after you make the call."

Chapter 118

"Sheriff, in here." Called Agent Blackmore. "We got a triangulation on the Marinelli calls. We think she's close but not in the county."

"How far?"

"Maybe 30 miles west of here."

Clancy looked up at the county map that hung over the dispatch desk. 30 miles would put her in Hannibal Missouri just across the river.

"You thinkink Hannibal Missouri?"

"Yeah, we call the local PD, set the sheet over."

"Good. Maybe we can roster next time she calls."

Clancy's private loin line rang.

"Sheriff Ryan."

Expecting Mary Elizabeth, Clancy was surprised by an older distinctive male voice.

"Sheriff Ryan, this is Vincent Marinelli. I thought we should talk."

"Are you behind what's been going down in my county?"

"No I'm not. I rarely stray from my own backyard."

"So your daughter is freelancing?"

"It would seem so. What she's into was done without my knowledge nor my permission."

"So you called to tell me exactly what?"

"I called to make inquiries as to the death of my son."

"Your son?"

"Yes. My daughter tells me that he died in your custody."

"Are you telling me that the man we knew as David Webster was your son?"

"Yes and it makes this personal between us."

"Did your daughter tell you how your son died?"

"No, just that he was in your jail when he died."

"I think she's trying to get you involved here. I'll tell you the truth. I have no reason to lie to you. Will you listen to me?"

"Yes."

"Your son was killed by a man who used to be our county attorney. A man we are actively seeking, this man was in league with your daughter, in fact was a college lover of hers. He's also thought to be responsible for the death of a Santos Fratelli, another of the men who came to town with Mary Elizabeth."

"Santos?"

"You know this man?"

"Yes, he's my nephew, my sister's kid."

"Then you should know that I have his brother in custody also, probably shop of the man we know is Webster."

"That's nuts, why would my son shoot his own cousin."

"That's a very good question. I don't know the answer to that. But look, we are small town in a small county in the middle of nowhere, and we don't need this kind of bull shit. You want to talk about getting personal. The man wanted for killing your son, I thought was my best friend. I've known in my entire life. I even had dinner with him last Sunday in his house. Since then, he's beaten his wife to a pulp, killed two men and kidnapped my fiancé. I've been shot at, almost blown up twice, and had my house shot to hell. Just this morning we stopped another attempt to kidnap my fiancé. You want to make a personal, I'm thinking it's personal."

"Sheriff, I don't operate this way. I'm a businessman not a thug. So I'm going to take you at your word that your department was not responsible for the death of my son "Good, but I still got four bodies in the morgue, two guys in jail, two guys in the hospital, plus a battered wife and several people around the County killing people. I need to put this all the rest. "

"What do you want?"

"I want my former best friend in jail. I want your daughter to turn yourself in, and I want to get married."

"Would you sell for two out of three?"

"No offense sir, but your daughter is the ringleader behind little bit of business. She's got to go down for some of it."

"Let me talk to her. Maybe we can reach an understanding."

"Yes, do that."

Chapter 119

Across town, Rebecca was trying to have a good time with her mother and her future mother-in-law. They for their part were getting along quite well. Rebecca was still shaken by all that had gone on. She couldn't help an overriding sense of impending doom and felt real fear for the first time since Chicago.

"What's the matter, Hon?" her mother asked.

"I'm still a little shaken after all that happened."

"You should eat something."

"Really not hungry mom."

"Why don't we go back to my house, we can relax there." Said Mrs. Ryan.

"Please, I'd like to get out of the public eye," Said Rebecca.

Mrs. Ryan waved her hand at Nick, who came over immediately.

"Yes Mrs. Ryan. What can I bring you."

"I was hoping you could tell the deputy to bring the car around to your backdoor. We'd like to leave as quietly as possible.

"The young doctor's not feeling well?"

"No, still a little under the weather I'm afraid."

"This is a bad business Dr. Whitmore. Please don't judge our town by this unfortunate business. I've been here all my life and I love it here."

"I'm not going to leave Nick. I'm just a little shaken that's all."

"That's good to hear. Bring the sheriff by when this all blows over, I'll fix you both something special, something from the old family recipes."

"I'd like that Nick."

Nick waved over a busboy, after talking quietly to him, the young man headed out the front door.

"Mrs. Ryan, will worry about the bill at another time. Please follow me."

"Thank you Nicholas. Always the gentleman."

"But of course."

Chapter 120

Clancy was looking over some case files when he heard a knock on his door. When he looked up, he saw Rebecca's father standing there.

"Hey Clancy could I steal a few minutes of your time."

"Sure John, come on in." Said Clancy think of for the break." What can I do for you?"

"Nothing really, with the woman off on their lunch date, I thought we could talk a little."

"You have said something in particular you want to ask me?"

"Naw, just be an overprotective father."

"I would be too if I was in your shoes."

"So you don't mind us talking a bit?"

"Not at all."

"You were a cop in DC for a while."

"Three years, don't much like big cities."

"They have their advantages and the disadvantages."

Clancy was hoping John Whitmore would get to the point of his coming in. He had an idea where it was heading. But figured he would allow Mr. Whitmore his future father-in-law to play it out.,

"Clancy, I've always hoped Rebecca would join me in my practice in Boston. She could make a name for herself there."

"It was her choice to come here and it will still be her choice when all this is over."

"Don't get me wrong here. I would never stand in her way. If this is what she wants then I'm all for it."

"So what are you really trying to tell me here?"

"I guess I'm just being he overprotective parent again. It was also quick. I want to be sure in my mind, that's all."

"I understand that, and yes, it was awfully quick. It's hard for me to explain, but this thing is real."

"That I believe Sir. You seem like a good man, Clancy. That's something in itself."

Clancy's private line rang again.

"Sheriff Ryan."

"So, do we have a deal."

"No. Even after we talked, you tried to kidnap Rebecca again. Now I got another one of your goons in jail and another one in the morgue. These family members to?"

"How'd you know about that?"

"Had a long talk with daddy this morning. I set them straight on why his son and his nephew are dead. He is not a happy man."

"What about my money?"

"Don't you mean my money."

"Look you Hicktown bastered. I want what's mine."

"Okay here's the deal. Turn yourself in, and bring Mike Billings with you alive and I'll see that you only spend 30 or 40 years in prison."

"Fuck You."

"Sorry, not gonna happen, never had a taste for skinny little girls."

Clancy hung up the phone before Mary Elizabeth could answer "Was that who was behind all the trouble in town?" Asked John.

"Yeah daughter of a New Jersey mob guy. Already got her brother, a cousin, and two other guys killed over what, money?"

Agent Blackmore stuck his head in the door, buthesitated when he saw John Whitmore,

" Come on in Dan,"said Clancy. This is Dr. John Whitmore Rebecca's father."

"Pleased to meet you Sir, Special Agent in charge, FBI, Dan Blackmore."

"FBI, here McAbee?"

"Came down on the Chicago to help Clancy. When your daughter was kidnapped it became a federal matter."

"Did you have something for me Dan?" Said Clancy.

"Yeah, it's definitely Hannibal. I sent Rodriguez and Shepard over in an unmarked Squad. It's a small town, maybe we'll get lucky."

"Hannibal is a tourist town, lots of people who don't live there."

"Will look anyway. Who knows, like I said maybe we'll get lucky."

The phone rang again.

"Sheriff Ryan."

"Hi, it's me," said Rebecca.

"Hi sweetheart, how did lunch go."

"Oh, okay, I guess."

"You sound a little down. What's the matter?"

"I guess I'm still a little spooked by all this."

"I'm sure, but it will all be over soon."

"I hope so. My father's there isn't he?"

"Yes."

"He's a good man, but he's always been a worrier. Kept a keen eye on us grow when were growing up.

"I respect that. It's the way I'd be if had any kids."

"Not if, when we have kids."

"Yes ma'am, when we."

That may Rebecca laughed a little. That may Clancy feel a little bit better.

"So how are the mothers getting along?"

"Like long-lost sisters. We may have to get married just so they can be friends."

"Do you need me to come home early?"

"That would be nice but I know you're very very busy."

"I'll see what I can do."

"It's not that important. I just need someone to hold me tight. Thought you might want the job."

"I do, give me an hour. The repairman should be gone by then we'll have the place to ourselves."

"Okay by then."

"By."

Chapter 121

Clancy looked up and saw John staring at him.

"Was she upset?" Asked John.

"Tired mostly, but yeah, she's upset."

"She came here to recover, more to get away from the city and all its hardness."

"I know what happened in Chicago."

"Then you can understand why I'm a little apprehensive now."

"Absolutely, she suffered than you think."

"No doubt, did you know she wanted to be a cop."

Clancy smiled and said," no I didn't."

"The yeah ever since she was a little girl."

"That explains all the forensic and medical examiner training."

"Yeah she thought she could be a cop and a doctor that way."

Clancy looked at his watch. It was nearly 4 o'clock in the afternoon.

"Why don't we get out of here. I don't have to stay and I'll bet Rebecca could use a little cheering up."

"Great," said John as he stood.

Clancy stopped by the office the feds were using to tell them he was leaving for a while.

"I'll call in as soon as I know where I'm goingto be." He said as he headed to the door. He almost made it before his phone rang again.

"Sheriff Ryan."

"Hello Sheriff, Vincent Marinelli."

"Hello Mr. Marinelli, what can I do for you now?"

"I've got you some information for you. I give you this information freely in the hopes that you will treat my daughter fair."

"Go on."

"I'll need your word of honor is a gentleman and is the high Sheriff."

"I am an honorable man. Always have been, always will be, but I can't promise you anything. I've never stepped outside of the law, and I never will."

"Good enough, the two guys who tried to take your young Dr. don't work for anybody out here. They work for Jimmy Cavalli."

"Cavalli? I thought he was in prison."

"He is, prison doesn't stop his kind of business."

"How do you know this?"

"I know people. Those guys were out of St. Paul, it was Cavalli's drug money that got stolen."

"How exactly does is help me?"

"Cavalli's an animal. As soon as he finds out his money was gone, he's gonna start whacking people. I don't want to lose my daughter to. If she's in with those guys, and doesn't come up with the money, the killer."

"I still don't see how this helps me or the case,"

"Mary Elizabeth and your former friend, are at the Riverview hotel room 411 on Chestnut Street, Hannibal Missouri."

"Alice," Clancy screamed, "Get me the chief of police in Hannibal. Missouri, now."

Alice nearly jumped out of her seat.

"Okay, but you don't have to scream."

"Just do it."

Clancy jumped from his seat, sprinted across the hall and stuck his head in the door of the FBI's temporary headquarters.

"Dan, we got an address on Marinelli and hopefully Billings."

The agent Blackmore was already on the phone to agent Rodriguez.

"I got Rieger Rodriguez almost there, I'm going to go over now to, you coming?"

"Hell yes, Alice, the chief's name?"

"Brooks, on line one." She called back.

"Chief Brooks, Sheriff Ryan here over Maccabee County Illinois."

"Yes Sheriff, good to hear from you. What can I do for you?"

"I've got to FBI agents heading your way. We have it on good authority that the people responsible for a series of Murder's here in McAbee are holed up in the Riverview hotel, room 411. You know it."

"Yes a flophouse down by the river."

"The FBI guys are still about 10 minutes out. The rest of the rest of us can get there for almost a half an hour. Anyway I can get a car over there to watch the place?"

"I'll do you one better. It's been a slow day here. I can put a couple of cars on it. Anybody in or out will be detained."

"That super"said Clancy. "I'll be there as fast as I can. Thank you."

"Don't think me were all in this together now," said Brooks as he hung up the phone.

"Alice."

"Yelling again."

"Get Hank on the phone, tell him what's going on."

"What about the SWAT boys, there still around."

"Call Capt. Andrews, tell him what's going down. See what he thinks."

"Done."

Agent Blackmore was already outside filling his truck with some very big guns.

Hank Brown slid into his space and said," What's up?"

"Looks like we got Billings and Marinelli over in Hannibal. Got the locals watching them. You want to come along?"

"Damn Skippy I do."

"Good, you drive. Full lites to get to the river."

"Let's go."

Clancy was about to jump into his squad when he saw John Whitmore standing outside on the sidewalk.

"I'm sorry John. This could be it. I gotta go."

John just nodded and said, " Call Rebecca before you go."

"Damn, I got a call Rebecca." He said as he got into the car.

"Make a quick," called agent Blackmore.

Clancy dialed his number, Rebecca picked up.

"I'm not be able to come home right away. We've got a solid lead that we've just got to follow up on."

"It's okay, I'm cooking something special so don't belong."

"I wish I could tell you when, but I'll try to be home soon."

"Okay, see you then."

Clancy hung up the phone and let out a long sigh.

"Going to have to get used to it if she's going to be married to a cop."

"I know."

Chapter 122

Clancy and Hank parked their squad car about a block away, not wanting to be seen. They didn't see any other police cars or the FBI guys. That didn't mean they weren't there.

Clancy and Hank walked slowly down the sidewalk keeping closeto the buildings. The Riverview set in the middle of the block, facing the river. It was an old, run down place that looked as if Mark Twain himself could have spent the night. Clancy counted four stories. That meant that their quarry was on the top floor.

As they were making their way down the street, A Hannibal city cop stepped out from a storefront and said," Sheriff Ryan, in here."

Clancy and Hank ducked into the store and found several more city cops. An older man in plain clothes step forward.

"Sheriff Ryan, I'm Chief Brooks. Good to meet you."

Clancy shook Chief Brooks hand and said, "good to meet you too sir. What if we got so far?"

"Well, there still in thier room. One of my guys saw a man carrying a tray of food about 10 minutes ago, so my guess is the eating."

"Has anybody seen the FBI guys?"

"Yeah," said one of the cops. "Two Feds parked west on First Street."

"The chief turned to one of his guys dressed in plainclothes and said.

"Casually walked down the street and give the feds a one up on what's going on and where we are."

"Right chief."

Five minutes later Agent Blackmore came through the door. After introductions were made agent Blackmore said. "This is your call chief. Your guys can do the takedown or we can call in HRT out of St. Louis. We could have them here in an hour."

"Let's do that, call your team in and will just wait. Will contain them and only move if either of them comes out."

When agent Blackmore went to make a call, Clancy filled chief Brooks in on the case.

"So, that's your County attorney up there?"

"Yep, a man I've known my entire life. This guy has dropped off the edge of reality and I need to know why."

"The feds are pretty good of that this kind of takedown. They don't want flight."

Blackmore came back in and said, "45 minutes, all we have to do is contain."

"We got the place surrounded. I don't see how they could get out." Said the chief.

"So we wait," said Clancy." I need to make a call."

Chapter 123

Up in room 411 things were not going so smoothly, Mary Elizabeth was mad as hell, and pacing the floor, cursing everybody and anybody.

"Will you come down will think of something."

'Shut the fuck or I'll kill you right here, you worthless piece of shit "

"Good idea, kill your only viable bargaining chip. Save me from having to spend the rest of my life in prison."

"Just shut up and let me think."

"Sure, you've done a bang up job so far."

"Oh and what about your brilliant idea of kidnapping the doctor. That was the stupidest thing you could've done. Now we got the feds to worry about."

"We should just take off, leave the country."

"Not without the money. We don't get anywhere without any money."

"That money is gone. You'll never see a nickel of it"

"We'll see. Check outside again, make sure were not made yet," Mike stood by the window and looked out. He saw nothing. Still, it seemed a little too quiet out there.

"I'm going to walk around the block, just to be sure."

"No, StAy put. The less seen the better."

"I'm going nuts, sitting out here all day. I'm leaving."

Mary Elizabeth pulled out a chrome plated 308 and pointed and Mike.

"That the fuck down you, ain't going anywhere."

Chapter 124

Clancy had to walk two blocks to find a working pay phone. The cell phone craze had to reach Maccabee County yet. That would all change as soon as the new cell tower was finished. Until then it was all payphones and police radios.

His first call was to the County dispatch office. He needed to know if Alice had gotten through to the states attorneys office and one could he count on a prosecutor.

Alice in her usual efficiency said that one was on its way.

The second call was to Rebecca. He had to tell her what was going on he felt he owed her that.

"Hello." Came the most pleasant voice he could imagine.

"Hi, it's me."

"Hi yourself," she sounded very tired. "Where are you?"

"I'm in Hannibal Missouri."

"Why?"

"We've got Mike and Mary Elizabeth cornered in a flea bag hotel. Were waiting for the FBI's HRT group to get here."

"HRT?"

"Hostage Rescue team. They specialize in getting people out alive, and really want these two alive."

"Mom and Dad are here. They think they're going to go home tomorrow."

"And?"

"They want me to go with them."

There was a long silence. Clancy didn't know what to say.

"Clancy, say something."

"I would just have to come get you."

"That's exactly what I said when I told them no."

"I know this is been rough on you, but it will end soon, I hope. Then you be able to see just how nice Maccabee can be."

"I don't think it's the town it's keeping the here. Even after all it's happened, I want to start a life with you. I'm in for the long haul if you'll have me."

"Have you? Are you kidding me? The thought of you leaving. I'm not think about that."

"I guess you're saying that you're stuck with me/"

"Yeah, the most beautiful, intelligent woman I've ever met." What a burden."

"Keep talking like that I just might wait up for you."

"If all goes smoothly I'll be home soon. If things go bad, I might be here a while. Get some sleep, we do have the rest of our lives."

Chapter 125

"I've got to get out of here." Said Mary Elizabeth. "I'm going to get a soda or something. You want anything."

"Yeah a soda would be nice."

Mary Elizabeth picked up the gun, placing it in through on a jacket.

"Locked the door behind me asshole and don't even think about leaving."

Mike locked the door behind the woman now hated. He had to get away. Nothing good since he call her with his plan to steal the Turner's drug money. She couldn't be happy with a few hundred thousand. Dollars. She brings in her aaahole brother and those two moron cousins. She was going to take over the the whole business, make millions. Where are they now? In a two bit flophouse, waiting for the cops to come get them.

"What a fucking," messy thought.

Chapter 126

As soon as Mary Elizabeth walked out of the elevator, she knew something was wrong. The lobby was deserted were just yesterday it was full of people. The old bag of bones behind the desk was replaced by a guy who looked like just walked off a college campus. Too young to clean and two well-dressed.

She smiled at him and asked for change for the pop machine. He fumbled around the drawers to the front desk but couldn't find the money drawer.

Time to go. She walked quickly to the elevator, could to the side and pulled out her gun, the elevator door closed without any trouble, but she knew they'd been made.

The man at the lobby desk picked up his two-way radio and said, "Chief, we've been made."

Chapter 127

Mary Elizabeth knocked on the door and waited for Mike to answer. When no answer came she tried to handle. Not locked. Mike was gone.

"Fucking Asshole." She said out loud." Can't trust anybody anymore."

She began packing things she planned to takewith her, when Mike came running into the room .

"There's cops everywhere."

"I know, they even have one behind the desk in the lobby."

"What do we do?"

"We get the fuck out of here."

"How?"

"Through the basement."

Chapter 128

The chief turned a Clancy and said. "My guy think she made them."

"I told you no one would believe him," said the old man who was usually at the desk." Now the getaway."

"How, we've got every entrance covered?"

"Nope."

"What you mean nope," asked Clancy.

"Not the basement. Got a passageway that leads to the river. Used to be a smugglers hole."

"Shit." Said Clancy as he ran out the door followed by Hank and two the Hannibal's finest

"Grab him to", said Clancy pointed that the old man'

"Who me? You're going to get me shot,"

Chapter 129

Mary Elizabeth and Mike Billings crept down the stairs trying to avoid the cop at the desk. Once they got past the first floor, Mary Elizabeth thought they had it made.

"This way." She said pulling Mike by the coat.

"Where are we going?"

"While you are off kidnapping the Sheriff girlfriend I was making sure we an exit strategy. I found an old tunnel that connects to the river. Must've been for smugglers or something."

"Don't you think they know about it?"

"Yeah probably, but they won't think we know about it."

Chapter 130

Clancy and Hank stood with the old man who had pointed out where the tunnel came up.

"Right there by the rocks."

As luck would have it, the FBI group HRT arrived. The HRT group is a squad of eight highly trained FBI agents, fully armored and ready to go anywhere anytime anyplace tjey were needed. The leader a hard looking ex-Marine name Lockport step forward.

"Agent Blackmore?" He askede he asked."

"Here," Said Dan.

"What's the situation?"

Before Dan could answer Cheif Brooks came running up.

"My guy at the desk just reported that two people, a man and a woman, headed down into the basement."

"Okay, were on." Said Davenport. "Chief, take your medicine secure the hotel.

Work your way down to the basement and cut off the entrance to the tunnel.

Pointing to the old man, he said." Take our friend here with you."

"I'm getting shot for sure now." He moaned.

"Cmdr. Lockport, bring your guys with us, we need to cover that tunnel exit.

Everybody started running at once. The HRT commander," yelled," Get the beacons." Two of his men stopped at the HRT vehicle and got out two of the largest flashlights anybody had ever seen.

"Put one of these in someone's eyes, they won't see for an hour." said one of the HRT guys.

Is the approach the tunnel entrance Dan signaled them to proceed quietly. The HRT group went instinctively two positions above and around the entrance. Deep in the tunnel,Clancy thought he could hear the shuffling of feet over uneven ground.

"We found the entrance to the tunnel in the hotel," came the report from the Hannibal cops. "Were heading in."

"Okay," said Dan." Lite the lamps."

The HRT group lit the beacons in the opening to the tunnel lit up like daytime. For HRT guy stepped out of the shadows pointing the guns at the surprise Mike and Mary Elizabeth. Mary Elizabeth turned and tried to run back up the tunnel only to see lights coming down the way that they had just come from.

"Drop your weapons and lay down face first on the ground."

"What do we do, what we do?" Mike cried.

"We surrender." Said Mary Elizabeth in a very casual voice.

"So this is it." Said Mike in almost a whisper. "Caught like a rat sewer."

Michael Billings layed down next to Mary Elizabeth Marinelli.

The HRT guys ran forward, kicked the gun away, and put restraining straps on both of them. No shots were fired and no one got hurt.

Clancy, Dan and Hank Brown, were standing in the rocks as HRT brought them out. Mike looked up at Clancy, but didn't say a word. All Clancy could think was what a sad day this was.

Mary Elizabeth was not so willing to be quiet. As soon as you saw Clancy she started to yell.

"You think this is over Sheriff. When my father finds out about this, he is going to rip your shit ass town to shreds"

"Your father was one who gave you up, Mary." He said, as he watched the color drained from Mary Elizabeth Marinelli's face.

"He, he wouldn't do that," She stammered. "He wouldn't"

"He would and he did. For as little as a promise not to hurt you."
Mary Elizabeth smiled. She knew who had won.

"Well Sheriff, what now?" Asked chief Brooks.

"We should let them sit in jail for a while. I'm sure Agent Blackmore will know if there will be any federal charges."

"We got Billings on kidnapping."said Dan. " We're going to have to think about any charges for Miss Marinelli. But your murder charges should go first."

"Are we going to have any problem extraditing them?"

"Naw." Said Chief Brooks. "We got a real friendly judge here. He'll send them over as soon as possible."

"Good," said Clancy. "I'm going home."

Chapter 131

By the time Hank dropped Clancy off at his house, it was well after mid-night.

The house was dark except for one light in the living room. Clancy let himself in as quietly as possible. Asleep on the couch with her foot propped up on several pillows, was the woman he was going to spend the rest of his life with.

He reached down and gently picked her up. She instinctively put her arms around Clancy's neck and snuggled in. He didn't think she even woke up. He laid on the bed and tucked her in.

As he stood looking at her sleepingin his bed, he couldn't help but be amazed that

this wonderful woman chose to stay with him. He resolved to make her life as good as he knew how.

Chapter 132

When Clancy woke up the next day, it looked like it was midmorning.

The clock said it was 10:30 and Rebecca was already gone. On his role and headed downstairs.

" About time you got up," said a smiling Rebecca." Coffee?"

"Sure, I really overslept. I got a call the station."

"Already did, I told them the high Sheriff was taking the day off."

"So you decided this all on your own did you?"

"Yes and Alice agrees with me. You need a day off, emphasize it's Saturday."

"Saturday, I really lost track of the days. Have your parents left yet?"

"No, actually on their way over to say goodbye."

"I'd better get a shower than."

Before Clancy went up for a shower he walked up behind Rebecca, put his arms around her waist and kissed her neck, Rebecca stopped what she was doing and said, "As soon as my parents leave Clancy Ryan, we have some serious unfinished business to take care of."

"As if I don't have enough pressure these days."

She had him in the shoulder.

"I'm never going to get used to you hit me so I guess I'll have to find some other way to make it stop."

"Oh yeah, what you do big boy."

Clancy tightened his grip around her waist, Picked her up off the floor and began to tickle her ribs.

"Clancy no, no," she squealed." I'm going to pee."

"I'll stop right after you promised to stop hitting me."

"I promise, okay."

"Doesn't sound so sincere."

"I swear, please Clancy I'm gonna to pee myself."

Clancy was holding her tight against his chest while she squirmed and squealed when she heard someone clear her throat. Clancy froze with Rebecca hanging in midair. There at the screen door looking at them like they just been caught naked in the backseat of a car not only Rebecca's parents, but his own mother as well.

"Tent pole."

"What?"

"Tent pole."

"Oh shit" said Clancy as he realize what she meant.

"Stall them." He said as he bolted up the stairs.

"Just let me get dressed," he yelled down to them.

Upstairs Clancy turned the water to the hypothermia setting, and jumped in. He dreamt dressed quickly and headed back downstairs.

"Clancy Ryan, whatever were you doing to this poor child?"

"Curing an illness." He said giving Rebecca sideways glance. She she returned his glance by wriggling up her nose at him.

"Clancy." Said John Whitmore. "I suppose Rebecca told you that we tried to talk her into coming back to Boston with us."

"Yep, she told me."

"I want to be perfectly clear about that. It was never about you son."

"It's pretty hard not to take it personally." Said Clancy, noting the use of the word 'son.'

"Can we chalk it up to an overprotective father, looking out for his only daughter. The see now that you are a good man, and will do right by Rebecca as her husband. We would be very proud to have you as our son-in-law."

"Thank you sir. It means a lot to hear you say so."

"Tammy and I have hopes that we will all be a great family together."

"I see no reason why that will be true." Said Clancy.

"Great." Said John." I have one small request of you."

"Shoot."

"Can I see the cars."

"Sure, come on outside."

"Clancy, honey," said his mother. "I've got to go to, I meeting with the ladies auxiliary."

"On a Saturday?"

"Yes dear, were deciding on how best to help Bea Billings."

"Shoot, I'd forgotten all about Bea."

Clancy grabbed the phone and dialed a familiar number,

"Hello Mayor, Clancy Ryan here."

"Hello Clancy. I heard of all about the arrests."

"Yeah I'm sure glad it's all over."

"So what can I do for you this morning?"

"I was hoping you could use your sway with the school board and have them offer Bea Billing the job as school librarian."

"You're kidding. Right?"

"Not on your life."

"But how could I after what happened?"

"Bea is a victim here Mayor, you'll be seen as a hero for stepping in."

"You think?"

"Why don't you ask your wife what she's doing for lunch today?"

"I already know what she's doing for lunch today. I've got to think about it."

"Fair enough. But think about this, you get this job for Bea, I won't run for mayor come the next election."

"You wouldn't."

"I can and I will."

"This is blackmail."

"Yes it is."

Rebecca leaned in close enough into the phone so the mayor could hear her and said," Mayor Ryan, got a nice ring to it don't you think?"

"Okay, okay, can start is and she's better."

Clancy turned to find the four people standing in his kitchen, staring at him with complete amazement.

"Now you have something to take your luncheon."

"How did you ever think of this son," said his mother.

"Mr. Stackhouse is 67 years old and wanted to retire last year. Bae Billings has a degree in library sciences from Southern Illinois University. Sounds to me like a perfect fit."

"I am truly impressed Clancy," said John.

'Thanks, lets goes see the cars."

Clancy and John went out to the garage to look at the cars, Mrs. Ryan took her leave. Rebecca and her mother sat together in the kitchen.

"That was pretty impressive." Said Tammy.

"Yeah, I'm a little surprised myself."

"So, you'll be happy here?"

"Yes I will."

"Have you talked about when you might be getting married?"

"No, not yet. But you and dad will be the first to know."

"He's a good man, Rebecca."

"I know."

They hugged and Rebecca had to choked back a tear.

"Let's go collect your father or also he'll be out there all day."

"I sure wish you could stay for a while."

"I do to, but it's time. Will be back soon enough and you're coming to Boston right."

"Maybe next month, after my ankle heals."

Mrs. Whitmore collected her husband, everybody said their goodbyes and they left.

As they were turning the last corner Clancy turned to Rebecca and said, just before they're out of sight, Clany said,   "About that unfinished business you spoke of."

Chapter 133

Clancy showed up at the station house bright and early Monday morning. From the time Rebecca's parents had left n they talkedu til 20 minutes ago he'd been with Rebecca. They made love, they talk they made love again. Clancy thought he could stay here all year.

That's if Hank Brown hadn't called to tell him that Mike Billings and Mary Elizabeth Marinelli, had waived extradition and would be back in town at 10 AM.

Clancy thought he could just stay home, but there was a lot to do before prisoners were transferred to McAbee. He still hadn't heard from the states attorneys office but a prosecutor and he had about 1 million reports the file. There was also the question about finding the money that had been the root of all this trouble.

"Sheriff," said Alice. "There's a man from the states attorneys office waiting for you."

"About time."

Clancy walked down to the waiting room and found a man that he alresdy knew.

"Ted Briscoe, when did you start working for the state?"

"About a year ago. Came down to new states attorney."

"This is great, it's good to see you. Are you to be the new prosecutor?"

"Just the advance man. I'll do the pulmonary arraignments. The states attorney wants to send a team of her very best down. Apparently she doesn't like traders. Plus there is the mob connection. The only problem we see is with Miss Marinelli."

"What do you mean?"

"A whole Lotta theory but not much evidence."

"She was behind this whole thing."

"You know it and I know it, but it's about what we can prove."

"No doubt daddy is going to send a high-priced legal team down here to help her out."

"No doubt. Where can I set up?"

"Why not Billings old office."

"Good enough, I'll get started."

Chapter 134

At 9:30 AM, Will Johnson parked his truck outside the courthouse. Clancy saw him pull in and went outside to find out what he was up to.

"These people tried to set me up to take the fall for Jake's murder. I wanted to make sure they knew I'm still here."

Soon other people begin to show up as he got closer to 10 o'clock.

At 9:55, Rebecca short showed up with Bea Billings in tow.

"This is turning into a circus," thought Clancy.

He had Junior moved the crowd across the street butallowed Willie, Rebecca and Bea stay.

At 10 o'clock Alice yell out the window that they were coming. How she knew this was anybody's guess. Sure enough, the states police cars came into the square and stopped right in front of the courthouse. Two cars with an orange clad prisoner eat in back each.

First out was Mary Elizabeth Marinelli, coughed and shackled, she looks small, may be a little lost. She didn't say a word is a took her inside.

Once she was inside the state troopers opened up the door to the other car and began to help Mike Billings out of the backseat.

"Clancy should have known to be trouble. He should have, but his romantic weekend with Rebecca had left him 100 miles away.

Clancy was looking at be. The pain in her eyes said everything. Of all the victims, she would suffer the most. Clancy thought he and Rebecca would have to be there for her.

Clancy was lost in his thoughts about how it about how it'd come to this when he heard Junior yelling.

"Not so high and mighty are you now, asshole?"

Clancy spell was broken. As he looked in the direction of JR. to see him nose to nose with Billings.

"Junior, backup away from the prisoner." Said Clancy.

Junior ignored him and went on ranting.

"Always acting so important, not so important now are you."

Junior was still right up in Mike's face. As a last gesture Junior spit in Mike's face, spun on his heels and started to walk away. Mike lunged at Junior, grabbed his gun and shot him twice in the back.

Mike began to wave the gun around, pointed everybody, Hank Brown who had just driven up in his car, came out with his gun drawn.

"Everybody just calm down." Yelled Clancy." What the hell you doing Mike. Hasn't there been enough of the shed for you."

"Fuck you Ryan. I'm sick and tired of you always being the fucking hero, you and that ass holeover there," he said pointing that will Johnson.

"Come on Mike give us the gun."

Hank was now pointing his gun right at Mike's had.

"Big tough Clancy Ryan, the football star. And Willie with all his grand daddy's money. The big man in town. Me just the tagalong little buddy . Clancy and will, all I ever heard of, Clancy and Will.

"And what about Bea, Mike. Why'd you have to put her in the middle of all this?"

"Don't be stupid. The whole town know she'd rather be with you. I was the second choice."

"That's not true." Cried Bea

"Shut up, bitch." He said, waving the gun at her.

"Mike, think about it. We can work this out."

"Sure, I'll just say I'm sorry and will all go back to work in the morning."

"Why Mike why?" Moaned Bea, now in full tears.

"Why not, it's my ticket out of this hellhole, away from all you hicks. Especially away from you Ryan. I so fucking hate you. Now you going to marry the new Dr.. The perfect couple, our very own Ken and Barbie. Well fuck that," he said as he swung the gun towards Rebecca.

Clancy was moving with him. Mike pointed the gun at Rebecca, who stood frozen in fear and pulled the trigger.

Clancy lunged at Rebecca, just as Mike shot the bullet hit him in his chest went through his long and Lodge near spine. The last thing he thought before he passed out was "Two shots."

Chapter 135

Clancy was so confused, he could hear talking but couldn't make out what anybody was saying. Someone was crying but he didn't know who.

"Who's doing all the crying."

All he heard was more crying. He opened his eyes and saw a face soaked with tears and ruined make up.

"Is that you making all that noise?"

"Yeah, so what," said Rebecca through the sniffles. She was clutching his hand in a death grip.

"Two shots."

"What?"

"I heard two shots."

Will Johnson leaned over and said," the second one was Hanks."

"Mike?"

"Dead."

"Junior?"

"Dead."

Clancy laid back on his pillow and sighed. "Damn, what a complete mess."

To Rebecca he asked, "What are you crying for?"

"You, you big ape."

"Why, what happened to me?"

Again it was Will," Well, to tell the truth, you died. Good thing the best doctor in the countywas standing right right behind.."

"Wh,at I got shot again?"

"Yep," said Will. "And the good doctor saved you."

"How long was I out?"

"Three days, they had to perform two operations to save your lung."

He felt bone tired. Tha last thing he saw before he fell asleep was a face smeared with makeup and wet tears.

Chapter 136

Clancy got stronger as in the days that followed. The event made the national news. 'Small-town Sheriff throws himself in front of a bullet to save the woman he loved. The first time he wanted to puke.

Everybody came by to see him. The governor, always aware of a photo op, came by to get his picture on the front page of USA Today, shaking the Clancy's hand from his hospital bed.

Enough. Five people were dead. Enough. Countless more lives were ruined. Enough. Clancy said 'no more'. He called Hank Brown and made him acting Sheriff, a role Hank tried to turn down.

Clancy said," If not you Hank, then who?"

"Okay." he said reluctantly. But it's only temporary right?"

"Yeah, I'm going to need some time here."

Later on Rebecca came by. He was so happy to see her, and for her part, she seemed happy to see him, but something was wrong.

"You going to tell me what's a matter."

"It's nothing."

"It's something, tell me."

"You could've died, you should have died. I'm never been so scared in my entire life, watching you bleed out on the sidewalk. If Will hadn't slapped me, Iwould have let you die. I couldn't move. I" her voice trailed off." I failed you."

"Don't you dare doubt yourself, I'm still here because of you. People freeze up all the time. That must've been a hell of a scene. What could you expect to do,

"I don't know. All my training and I felt helpless."

"Objectivity is what we save for strangers."

"Boy, are you write about that. So where do we go from here?"

"Well if you can spring me from this hospital, we should find us a small church."

"Church? For what?"

"A marriage ceremony."

"We elope, my mother kills us."

"Let her have her day while we have ours."

Epilogue

One week after Mike Billings died on the streets of his hometown, he was laid to rest, only Clancy, Rebecca, and will Johnson join Bea and her two boys.

The last words Mike spoke would huant Clancy for the rest of his life.

Chief Deputy Thomas Thomas Junior's funeral had taken a place the day before. It was attended by hundreds of people including representatives of nearly all of the County sheriffs in Illinois. Nothing was said about the fact that his own stupidity is what got him killed.

Two weeks after the shooting Mary Elizabeth Marinelli walked out of jail a free woman. There was no direct evidence linking her to any of the murders and the charges they were able to pin on her, were dropped after she agreed to testify against her own cousin.

Alberto Fornelly was convicted of second-degree murder and sentenced to 20 years to life.

About mid-November Jimmy Tucker walked into the county courthouse and knocked on Clancy's door.

"You got a minute' Sheriff."

"Sure Jimmy, come on in."

"I come to say goodbye, I'm leaving town. Moving back up to St. Paul."

"Can't say I'm sorry to see you go."

"With Jake gone and the guys scattered there's nothing left for me here."

"You going to stay out of trouble?"

"Who's to say, at least still water is better than Joliet."

"I wanted you to have this." He said, as he handed Clancy legal sized folder." It's all legal, signed and sealed. You want to bat with my parole officer. You didn't have to do that."

"I couldn't see you going back to prison for getting the hell beat out of you".

"Thanks anyway. Watch your back, Sheriff," then he left.

Inside the folder was a signed transfer of ownership and the deed to 238 acres of prime McAbee farmland. Jimmy had given Clancy the farm.

Why would Jimmy Turner give the farm to Clancy? He just couldn't figure it out. Then like a lightning bolt from heaven, he thought,

'The missing money.'

The end

www.ingramcontent.com/pod-product-compliance
Lightning Source LLC
Chambersburg PA
CBHW071413200726

48294CB00002B/386